Hezekiah Butterworth

Boys of Greenway Court

A tale of the early days of Washington

Hezekiah Butterworth

Boys of Greenway Court
A tale of the early days of Washington

ISBN/EAN: 9783337088392

Printed in Europe, USA, Canada, Australia, Japan

Cover: Foto ©Andreas Hilbeck / pixelio.de

More available books at **www.hansebooks.com**

A foot race at Greenway Court.

THE
BOYS OF GREENWAY COURT

A Tale of the Early Days of Washington

BY

HEZEKIAH BUTTERWORTH
AUTHOR OF
IN THE BOYHOOD OF LINCOLN, THE LOG SCHOOL-HOUSE ON THE COLUMBIA
THE ZIGZAG BOOKS, ETC.

NEW YORK
D. APPLETON AND COMPANY
1896

CONTENTS.

iii

iv

CONTENTS.

LIST OF ILLUSTRATIONS.

THE BOYS OF GREENWAY COURT.

CHAPTER I.

A SURPRISE.

"OLLIE set that shoe, and you would know the name of that horse if the shoe were to be found fifty years from now."

"Yes, the Quaker blacksmith does his work well. Every shoe he sets bears the name of the horse."

A company of Virginians were gathered at a ford across a stream between Chesapeake Bay and the Potomac River not far from where the town of Harper's Ferry now stands. They were the owners or overseers of the great plantations that lay upon the broad arms of the Chesapeake Bay. They were holding a temporary cattle market and fair, and there had been a horse-race.

A part of the men were from Lord Baltimore's colony, or Maryland. The people of that section of the country where Winchester, Va., now is had been in attendance, and men had come from the Virginian plantations as far away as Williamsburg.

It was about the middle of the eighteenth century. The Indian troubles were beginning to cause alarm in the settlements on the Chesapeake. The long contest between the English and the French for the mastery of the continent was impending. The English settlements in the French territory of the Ohio were a menace to the peace of the country, and were preparing the way for the long and bloody contest known as the French and Indian War. The French were at this time masters of the larger part of the continent, the Canadas, the Lake region, and the vast territory beyond the Mississippi known as Louisiana. The Indians as a nation were their friends. Had the French held the country, it is probable that the Indian tribes would not have been almost extinct to-day.

Most of the land of Virginia at this time was a vast forest. There were great tobacco plantations on the waterways to the Chesapeake, of which the town of Alexandria was a part. The colony of Virginia numbered some seventy thousand inhabitants, and these had acquired much wealth and distinction under the vigorous and romantic administration of Governor Spottswood, then deceased.

It was one of those serene days that fall on the hills and woods of the Potomac in early autumn. The air seemed like a vast loom of light weaving the golden fibres of the sun. The Potomac lay glassy, without a ripple. The high hills afar were tinged with fall colors and were dreaming in the sun. The quiet of the day carried with it a sense of security. Not a breath of wind suggested that the world was not everywhere at peace. The men who were holding the fair lay outside of the booths and tents, smoking in the bright mellow air, bartering, talking English politics, and telling provincial stories. Their horses were tied to the trees, with baskets of grain before them. Collie, a Quaker blacksmith who marked horse-shoes with the name of the horse shod, was being discussed, when a puff of smoke arose from one of the hills in view, curling slowly upward in the clear air.

The men started.

"Indians," said one of the traders unconcernedly.

"Friendly, I hope," said another, an old man by the name of Bustle, whom they called major. The major was greatly afraid of Indians.

The eyes of the traders turned in the direction of the smoke. The air was still and clear. The bantering talk was resumed after a little silence.

"Collie set that shoe, and——"

"What is that?" suddenly asked a tobacco merchant, starting up.

Not far away there was a gleam of flints and feathers in the air, and a sound as of flying voices.

"Birds," said one.

"Arrows," said another.

"An Indian fishing party," ventured a third.

The air was breathlessly still. The smoke curled up like a spiral stair. Occasionally an impatient horse stamped and pawed the ground. The sun was slanting and the shadows were growing long.

A little apart from the camp was a beautiful bay mare, that from time to time whinnied and tried to break her tether.

"That horse acts strangely," said one of the men.

"Just been separated from her colt," answered another. "She's thinking of home."

"Did you ever hear the old Scottish story of 'The Jolly Harper Man'?" asked one of the Virginians, a young man named Rouzé.

"No," said several voices.

"It may be true or not, but it shows the instinct of motherhood in animals, and I will tell it to you."

The men gathered around the speaker, for he was an excellent story-teller. He began:

"'Twas long ago in old Scottish times, when the king's stables were on the Border."

"What king's?" asked an English pioneer.

A yell pierced the air. The men started to their

feet. The horses trembled. The bay mare broke her tether and, whirling round and round, plunged into the forest. She belonged to a young man from Winchester by the name of Lawrence and lived on a plantation far north among the hills. It was this horse that Collie had shod.

"Boy, go after her," said a tall planter from Fredericksburg. Mr. Lawrence had gone down the road a little way. "And don't you lose her or leave her. Be quick."

The boy's name was Harry Mendell, and he will form a conspicuous character in our story.

"It is not my horse, sir," said the boy.

"That has nothing to do with the case. I am master of the fair. Stop her, and don't you lose her or leave her, whatever happens. This is a scare, and not a fight."

"A s-c-a-r-e!" The words sawed the air. It was the voice of old Major Bustle. He was a gouty man, but he seemed to be dancing and to have lost his senses. He looked up.

"Not up—we can't go up, colonel." He addressed the master of the fair. "Nor down, colonel." The earth was surely solid beneath him. "And there is the river." He gave a nervous jump. "And *there* is . the *inemy.*"

As he uttered the last word, the head of a real

2

warrior darted out from behind one of the trees.   The
Indian drew his bow.

The frantic old man cried "Help!"   In his nervous
terror he turned round his wig.   The Indian had
never seen a wig before, and thinking that the major
had broken off the top of his head, he stood motionless
with wild eyes, as frightened as the old man himself.

"Boy, go," said the master of the fair.   The boy
obeyed, leaving the camp in terror, and following the
animal by the sound of the breaking dry wood bushes
and scattering leaves which was made in her flight.

The men of the camp, growing more and more terrified, looked hither and thither.   Nothing but the
forest and the river were to be seen, except the one
Indian who had marked the major.   Whence had
come the great cry?

It came again.   And nearer.   All the trees seemed
to send forth in concert a wild, piercing voice.

"The war-whoop!" said a Virginia colonel.   "To
our horses!"

"We are all dead men!" cried the major, still step-
ping up and down.

Then came a flight of arrows.   The great trees
seemed to be changed into animated warriors.
Plumes, dark hands, and twanging bows darted from
behind their trunks.

The men on the Maryland side of the Potomac fled

down the Baltimore road. The Virginians turned their faces toward the road that led down to the ford of the Potomac. It was a woody, embowered way, and the question arose in all minds whether the river could be safely crossed in view of the supposed enemy.

"Horses!" shouted the colonel. "To the ford!"

The Virginians were seized with a panic. They were unarmed, and they saw that their only safety was in flight. The major leaped like a boy upon the first horse he could find, saying, "We need not *all* be lost." Several others did the same, and following the example of the old man, they vanished like the wind.

This unexpected turn of affairs compelled some of the men to exchange horses. It was but the work of a few moments. The Indians, seeing their vantage, suddenly leaped out from their hiding-places behind the trees, and rushed laughing and leaping into the abandoned camp, turning somersaults and shooting their arrows into the air.

Indians laugh little, but a comical sight here amused them. As they looked down the road, they saw one horse flying away and plunging down into the forest with two riders upon his back, and in this manner spattering across the ford. The Indians were enemies to the English colony of Virginia, but they were not on the war-path now and meant only to cause an alarm, and the flight of the two men on one horse filled them with savage delight and they burst into wild, derisive laughter.

One of these two men was a tall planter whose fine horse had run away at the first alarm, and which Harry Mendell had been sent to find.

It was nearly night. The sun like a red arch flamed over the western hills. The shadows were growing cool and long. A heavy, fresh odor rose from the forests. The night birds were calling in the sky, and the sounds of home-flying birds and home-going animals filled the forests with a new sense of life.

The men all found the forest roads and made their way toward their homes, some to Winchester, some toward Alexandria, others toward Fredericksburg, and a few toward Williamsburg. A part of them expected to stop at a roomy forest tavern not many miles away, and to ride home in the morning. These lived on the west side of the Potomac.

Poor Major Bustle, of this party, was fearfully shaken in mind and body, but most of the men with him began to laugh and joke over the comical side of the affair, now the danger was past and they felt that they were not being pursued and that no harm had been meant.

"Collie set that silver-tipped shoe," said one of the

men, resuming the conversation with which our story begins.

"Where do you suppose she is now? It was rather unfair to the boy, to send him to find her amid a scare like that. If the major was so shaken up, what ought to be expected of a boy like him? Harry is a true-hearted fellow, if his mother is queer; an honest fellow, true as steel."

"There's no knowing when or where he will find the mare. She's just been separated from her colt, and is heady."

"A splendid animal, and it pleased young Lawrence to have Collie put upon her that silver-tipped shoe. I suppose the name of *Gay* is upon all her shoes. But that is neither here nor there. Say, colonel, what was that story about 'The Jolly Harper Man' that you were about to tell?"

"I am in no mood to tell an odd story like that after what has happened. My ears! I can hear that Indian yell now. We may hear another at any time. I fancy that I can see something bobbing in every bush."

"You will tell us that story some other day?"

"Yes, some Christmas night at Greenway Court. It is just the story for a merry-making."

We shall hear of the colonel and his story again.

The forest grew dark. There was one portion of

the road which was covered with vines and which was called The Shadow of Death. A white owl in the trees startled the nervous horses and threw the fidgety major again into a fright.

The maples flamed on the hillsides in the clearings as the moon rose. A part of the men turned toward Winchester, a part rode on the winding way in view of the Potomac. At last a light gleamed in the distance. It was the forest tavern. The travellers felt safe now, and even the major became light-hearted again.

"I wouldn't have believed that I could have been so frightened," said the latter. "It makes one know himself to hear an Indian yell! May I never hear the like again. I was born to stay at home."

Lanterns were swinging to and fro in front of the inn. Negroes were waiting to care for the horses. A hot supper was over the great red fire.

But Harry Mendell—where was he?

CHAPTER II.

"THE TWO GEORGES."

ARRY MENDELL left the strange scene of terror and mystery and comical stampede, to follow the sound made by the retreating horse, that he might capture the animal. He came upon her at the bank of the river, under the Maryland hills. She seemed about to plunge into the water from a bank a few feet high.

"Whoa, Scatter-hoof," said Harry, applying a name of doubtful credit to the animal, in as mild a tone of voice as he was able to command.

The mare paused, arched her neck, and pawed the earth. She was a beautiful creature, but there was a frenzied look in her eye as she threw her head up into the air and shook it.

Harry approached her, seized the loose bridle, patted her on the neck, and leaped upon her back. Mr. Lawrence, to whom she belonged, was a lawyer, on whose broad estate to the far north of Winchester among the hills the Mendells had their little home.

Mr. Lawrence had brought her to the Market Fair and races. What was Harry to do? It was clear to him that it was his duty to ride the animal home whatever might be the peril.

A sad place was his own home in a little clearing of the great Lawrence estate. His poor father was an invalid, and his mother, who was naturally one of the best and most tender-hearted women, was "queer at times" and a "little touched in mind," as the people were wont to say. Her love for Harry was very strong, and her pride in his honor and character seemed to be the one joy of her life.

During her "queer" spells she wished to be alone and to speak to no one. "You cannot understand it, Harry," she would sometimes say, "and I hope that you never will. I cannot tell you of the dark thoughts I struggle against when I have my spells. I pray all the time, and I would pray to die were it not for you, Harry. My boy, you do pity me, don't you? Bear with me, for I am your mother, and I do the best I can."

Harry loved his mother, but he could not understand her strange moods. He would sometimes say impatiently, during her silent days, "Mother, what does make you act so?"

"I cannot help it, Harry; if you knew how I struggle against myself you would not blame me, but pity me. You will think of me differently when you are old."

His father and mother were common work-people on a great plantation near the Winchester Hills. Harry had come to the Potomac to-day in a provision wagon, for the fair, with a party of gentlemen from Winchester. He had become noted as an expert rider among the North Winchester farmers, and as he drove a road team prudently he was selected to accompany this party.

His own horse had been seized in the fright; by whom he did not know. His wagon and its remaining provisions were left to the Indians. He drew the rein and attempted to turn the horse toward the upper ford that led to the North Virginia road. But she would not turn in that direction. She was bent on going south instead of north as if to some force that led to the south road to the Shenandoah.

Harry had won a good name for skill with animals. He had, as a rule, a peculiar influence over them. He was very kind to them and careful of them. He seemed to know how to anticipate their wants and to win their confidence.

"Now, Scatter-hoof," he said to Gay, and he drew the rein again firmly. But the horse refused to turn. Down the south road of the Potomac she was bent on going. She stood looking wistfully over the river, and whinnied in an excited but almost fretful tone. She knew the whole country well, and seemed to want to cross the river, but to the south and not to the north.

"That sounds human," thought Harry. "What is the matter with you, Scatter-hoof?" repeating again the odd name to Gay. He gave her the rein, and she slowly, but as it were doubtfully, walked along the bank of the river toward the south.

Suddenly she stopped, looked across the river, and whinnied again. Harry drew the rein with all the strength that he could command to turn her in the direction of the north ford that led to the Winchester road. But she stood as firm as a horse of bronze. She would not be driven that way.

The sun had gone down, leaving a sky of red embers. Light evening breezes rustled among the forest leaves. There were black clouds in the sky, and the hunter's moon rose broad and golden as a night sun and poured her reflected light over the great forest, soon to be darkened by clouds.

There had been a wild autumn storm recently, and the banks of the stream were broken. Near the place were the ruins of a temporary wooden bridge which had been washed away. Harry thought of his home, which was far off, of the abandoned wagon, and the dangers that might follow the events of the day. He tried again to turn the horse, but in vain.

"She is afraid of the Indians," he thought.

Then a darker thought came into his mind. It was of his mother, who was now under the influence of one of her melancholy "spells." He knew that his failure to return with the rest of the party would excite her, that she would not sleep, that she would be likely to wander about the plantation, as one dumb or chattering.

The horse began to move on again, but close to the broken banks of the river, stopping and looking over to the other side.

It grew dark. There were peals of thunder and the wind began to rise. What was he to do, homeless, supperless, without a human being near? Leave the horse and seek the road? He had a tender conscience. He had been ordered not to leave the animal, and to him to obey a command of duty was more than life, and to fail in duty something worse than death. His unfortunate mother was a religious woman, and she had schooled him to the highest and keenest sense of honor. "Harry, you must not do that to save your right hand," was a common expression with her when the boy brought a question of right or wrong to her for decision. "If you doubt a thing to be right," she used to say, "it is wrong. To lose right is to lose everything, and life without honor is a blight and disgrace. Be true to the best that is in you—always be true to that, my boy."

"Whatever impairs the tenderness of your conscience," she would often say, "and lessens your moral power, that to you is *sin*. Be true to the best that is in you."

Harry resolved not to leave the horse. Hungry, with the darkness of a storm gathering over him, he yet determined to obey the order given him. But the horse would not obey. Suddenly she turned toward a high bank of the river. Harry pulled the rein violently, but she kept on her course toward the high bank.

A man came down from the bank in the partial darkness, swinging a lantern. Harry saw the lantern before he discerned the man and thought it was the light of a house.

As the lantern approached he shouted.

"Sho!" said the man. "Whar you come from, shore?"

"From the fair."

"Whar you gwine?"

"I want to go to the North Virginia road. I am from Winchester."

"Sho', now, this am no way to No'f Winchester, boy. Foller me up no'f toward the ford. You must cross

the ribber. You can't cross the ribber down here,
boy. Sho', you're lost, sure. I am gwine up no'f.
Foller me."

"The horse won't turn."

"Sho', boy, I'll turn her. But I can't stop long,
I'm sent for. I'm ole Joe. Just ole Joe."

Old Joe took the mare by the bridle and turned
her toward the northern way down which she had
come. "Now foller me, boy."

Old Joe started forward, swinging his lantern.
The mare took a few steps forward, then turned
again.

Joe looked behind.

Harry pulled the rein with all his strength, but to
no purpose.

"Sho', boy, how that horse does act! She's no
good, onery like. I don't know what you'll do. I'd
help ye, but I's sent for."

Harry pulled the rein again. The mare rose on
her hind feet.

"Sho'," said the old negro, "I'm sorry. You'll
hab to trust in Providence, sure. I'm sent for. I
must hasten on. It gwine to storm for sure."

The old man plodded forward, swinging his lantern.
The horse seemed trying to look over the river in
the rapidly growing darkness. She went up the high
bank, and then began to feel her way down. She

seemed to be in a beaten path and to know the place
and the way.

A new sense of terror filled the heart of the boy.
What was happening? The horse seemed walking
upon the water. Was he dreaming? Had he lost his
senses? Was the horse enchanted or performing a
miracle? The darkness deepened. He could hardly
see.

The rim of the moon broke through a rift in the
cloud, and—could he believe his eyes?—there was
water all around him, and he could look down into
the depths of the river below him! He gasped in
terror and exclaimed, "Heaven save me for my
mother's sake!"

At last the horse stood still. The moonlight
streamed out again through the billows of cloud. He
looked behind. Water! He looked down. Water!
He saw the shore in the distance across the water.
The horse seemed pounding her feet against some
hard substance, but there was no bridge. The horse
appeared standing as in solid water in the middle of the
Potomac. A strange sound for such a situation fell
upon his ears. It was like the clinking of a loose
shoe against an iron spike. He heard it again and
again, but there seemed to be nothing under him or
around him but water.

Then, amid the darkness, the horse appeared to be

The horse seemed standing on solid water in the middle of the

sinking. Harry's feet were immersed in water, but only for a moment. Soon the horse seemed to rise up as into the air, and to be on land again. The sound of a horseshoe striking against a spike ceased. The horse was moving rapidly. The moon broke through the clouds. What had happened? Where was he? He had in some unaccountable manner crossed the river. The horse limped as if lame. What had injured her feet?

A gleam of fire broke the gloom. At some unknown distance ahead there was a camp. The horse hurried toward the spot, stopped and whinnied.

"Stop thar!" shouted the voice of a negro who was called Tom. "Who comes here?"

"I am Harry Mendell."

"Where's you gwine?"

"I am escaping from the Indians."

"The Indians—for the lan's sake! The Indians! Let me rouse Massa Washington!"

"Who is he?"

"Massa George Washington, de boy surveyor! Ain't you never heard o' *him?* He and George Fairfax am surveying here for de lord. This is Fairfax place, and de two Georges are out surveying, George Washington and George Fairfax. De Indians! De hebbens! Wot you say?—de Indians!

De prophets and 'postles sabe us now! Do I hear my ears? The Indians!"

"Surveyors?" asked Harry.

"Yas, for the ole lord."

"For the *old* lord?"

"Yas, for ole Lord Fairfax of Greenway Court. Don't you know? Whar your senses gone? What am de matter, chile?"

The two young surveyors whose camp Harry had thus entered bore the name of George. The older was George William Fairfax, of Belvoir, as a grand plantation was known that lay near the Mount Vernon estate on the Potomac. His father was the Hon. William Fairfax, a man of liberal education, high character, and great wealth, who had served with honor in the British forces of the East and West Indies and had been governor of New Providence, now commonly called Nassau. This gentleman had come to Virginia to manage in part the immense estates of his cousin, the famous Lord Fairfax, the heir of Lord Culpepper, who had received the Virginia grant from Charles II.

The young man was a cousin of the great Lord Fairfax, Baron of Cameron, whose estates embraced the Northern Neck, as the land between the Potomac and Rappahannock was called, and the Shenandoah Valley.

The rich old Lord Thomas Fairfax was a remarkable character. He was between fifty and sixty years of age at the time, a man of giant frame, gray eyes, and aquiline nose. He had been educated at Oxford, had been in the military service, had aspired to literature, and it is said that he had written articles for Addison's *Spectator*.

His life reads like a fiction. In the height of a brilliant London career, he had fallen in love with a lady of beauty and rank, offered himself to her, and had been accepted. The day was appointed for the wedding, the house prepared for the wedded life, when the lady suddenly changed her mind. She had received another proposal of marriage, and one more in accordance with her feelings. She had doubtless found a handsomer man, which it would not have been hard to do. Her fickleness changed the great lord's life. He wished to leave gay society forever, and to go to the Virginia forests that had been granted to his ancestor by Charles II. He shunned polite society ever after the day that brought him the disappointing refusal, but he still liked the society of young men, planters, and pioneers. He was known to many by another title, the Baron of Cameron.

He came to his great estates in Virginia and at first resided at Belvoir with William Fairfax, his cousin and agent. He resolved to erect a great castle or

3

manor-house in Virginia, and there live as a forest
lord, amid fine stables and lodges, with a great retinue
of servants.   He built a large, low house, with a long
veranda, and called it Greenway Court, intending it
as a temporary residence only.   But his grand castle
or manor-house was never built, and Greenway Court
became his permanent home.   He there lived in an
easy style of hospitality, and long after the present
time died there at the age of ninety-two.

He had the finest dogs in the country.   His hunting parties became famous.   His love of hunting
caused him to gather around him young hunters and
foresters.   These he formed into a cavalry company
during the war with New France.   They were among
the gallant boys of Greenway Court.

George William Fairfax, the young surveyor, was
a cousin of the old hermit lord.   The other George
belonged to the historic family of Washington.   He
was a few years younger than George Fairfax and
was hardly more than a boy.   It was he whose virtues
as well as military prudence won the cause of freedom and independence for the American colonies, and
who received the name of the " Father of his Country."
It is our purpose to give you an early view of his
history in this story and show you how his character, that became the hope and strength of America,
was formed and grew.

George Washington was the son of Augustine Washington (born 1694) and Mary (Ball) Washington, and was born in a pioneer homestead on Bridge's Creek, Virginia, near the Potomac River, on February 22d, 1732. The primitive farm-house where his infancy was passed commanded a view of the Maryland shore and was very beautiful in situation. It had four rooms on the ground-floor, other rooms in the attic, and great chimneys after the Southern style at each end. A stone placed there by George W. P. Curtis marks the spot to-day.

Not long after his birth his father removed to an estate near Fredericksburg. The house was similar in appearance to the one on Bridge's Creek and overlooked the lovely Rappahannock meadows.

The boy was sent to school to an old field schoolhouse. His early teacher's name was Hobby. This man was an odd character, and dug graves as well as instructed children. His next teacher was his brother, Lawrence Washington, who had returned from a course of education in England. He had become an officer under Admiral Vernon, from whom Mount Vernon, the historic Washington estate on the Potomac, received its name.

Lawrence Washington returned to Virginia in 1742, when George was some ten years of age. He was a half-brother of George and became greatly attached to

him.   He married Anne Fairfax, the daughter of Hon.
William Fairfax, the agent of the estates of the great
Lord Fairfax, Baron of Cameron.   Anne Fairfax was
a sister of George William Fairfax and passed her
early life at Belvoir.

The father of George Washington died on April
12th, 1743, when only forty-nine years of age.   George
was then eleven years old.   The boy lived at times
with his mother near Fredericksburg; at times with
his brother at Mount Vernon and with William Fairfax at Belvoir.   He became intimate with George
William Fairfax, and the two Georges were welcome visitors to old Lord Fairfax at Greenway Court.

Washington studied surveying while yet a boy, and
acquired a reputation for thoroughness and accuracy
in the profession.   The old lord liked to have him as
a member of his household at Greenway Court, and
employed him, as we have said, to survey his farm of
some ten thousand acres and his great estate of
nearly six millions of acres, a part of which is now
known as the Shenandoah Valley.

In these surveys the two Georges were sometimes
companions, and as such we meet them here.   Old
Lord Fairfax, if he were a giant and homely, with
his great head, gray eyes, and long nose, was a most
generous and hospitable man.   He loved to entertain
visitors, to tell stories, and to listen to stories of the

country, of the Indians, of the bush-rangers and the pioneers. Greenway Court became a most delightful resort of the Virginians and of the English travellers.

The old lord liked Greenway Court and the noble mountain and valley scenery which it brought to view. He loved the open air. What could better atone for the great wrong that he had suffered than life on the Northern Neck, as his estate between the two rivers was called, and in the majestic mountains of the glorious Shenandoah, where he had made his home!

He was a stanch royalist. To him these regions of beautiful rivers and forest-covered mountains were to be developed for the English king. The throne of England in his view was as sacred as though it were divine. He never dreamed that his young and manly visitor, George Washington, the intrepid surveyor, would one day lift his sword against that throne and sever the colonies from the English crown, and establish on the earth a new order of government by the people.

No, those were serene, chivalrous days of Greenway Court, where the old English games were played and the choicest stories, old and new, were told. Birthdays here were bountifully celebrated, and Christmas, with English hospitality and wonderful

story-telling, was an event long to be remembered.
The lord of the Shenandoah, if he had been disappointed in love, was a merry old man, and cheerful
places were the great rooms under the long, sloping
roof and veranda of Greenway Court.   And gallant
were the *boys*, as the young men were called, who
gathered there.

When Harry awoke in the morning he found the
old negro standing beside him.

"Boy," said Tom, "your hoss ha' gone.   For sure,
he dum am.   He dum am.   I looked for 'im ebbery-
where.   What kine of a hoss can dat be, sure!   Dar
was a dreadful rain near midnight, and I allows dat
dat animal went off in de storm.   How de win' did
blow!   We's all gwine to Greenway Court dis
mornin', and you'll hab to go wid us, widout yer hoss,
sure, you will now, unless you can find de onery
animal.   I speck dat hoss am cunjured."

Harry arose and went out into the bright mists
of the morning air.   Tom had spoken truly.   The
mare was nowhere to be seen or found.

CHAPTER III.

GREENWAY COURT.

THE two Georges rode through the forest on horses followed by two colored men on foot and by Harry, who wondered what next would befall him, and whose thoughts were of his poor mother and unhappy home.

It was a bright morning after the storm. The road wound under green trees like tents of crimson and gold, and the sun blazed on the wet shining leaves. Blue-jays were calling here and there, and squirrels were running to and fro amid the brown branches. The road was bestrewn with fading ferns, and little ponds of water stood in the hollows.

Harry followed silently. The loss of the horse gave him a heavy heart, for somehow he felt that it involved his honor. He had done the best he could. He had been true to his best self and a hero, but appearances were against him. Who would believe his true story?

The journey was long; the party encamped over night on the way.

From a hillside at last he saw the smoke of a low chimney and the sloping roof of a great forest home. There was a loud barking of dogs as the party came up to the great portico of a large house in English cottage style which had already become famous. It was Greenway Court.

An old gentleman, a visitor from Philadelphia, sat on the veranda, leaning on a cane. Near the house were a dozen slaves or colored servants, two of them old men and the rest women and children.

"Well, George," said the old Quaker to the younger Fairfax, "whom hast thou brought home with thee this fine morning? Speak up, boy, and tell us thy name." He had turned to Harry.

"Harry Mendell, sir."

"And where dost thou live, my young man?"

"Near Winchester, sir. Among the Northern hills."

"That must be a good place—a very good place. But what errand brings thee here?"

"No errand, sir. My horse ran away and carried me into the camp of the young surveyors."

"Your horse?"

"No, a horse that I was asked to catch and keep."

"Is that so?" said the old man, looking toward the two Georges suspiciously and striking his cane on the floor. "And where is the horse now?"

"I have lost her, sir."

The old man pounded his cane again on the floor and looked puzzled. The servants gathered around the veranda with wide-open eyes.

"Master George," said the old gentleman to young George Fairfax, "does this new acquaintance of thine speak the truth?"

"He came into our camp night before last with a fine horse, according to Tom's statement, just before the shower. The next morning no such animal was to be seen. But there certainly came a strange animal into our camp that night."

"Tut, tut," said the old man, shaking a silver snuff-box—"tut, tut, that sounds rather queer." He took a pinch of snuff, and leaning on his cane asked: "What made the horse run away?"

"The Indians."

An old black woman named Nancy and called Nance who was listening, all eyes, gave a loud howl and turned her face upward. This terrified the young colored children, who were now all ears. The startled woman bent herself almost double and stood shaking her turban.

"The Indians! Tut, tut, tut, tut, my young man, how came they to frighten the horse?"

"They yelled the war-whoop."

Poor old Nance started up and flung up her arms.

"We'll all be dead now, sure's ye're bawn. I heerd the owl screechin' and screechin' in the blasted pines last night, and I dreamed——"

"Be quiet," said the old man firmly. "I am questioning the boy. Where did you see the Indians?"

"At the horse fair."

"On the Potomac?"

"On the Potomac, sir; on the other side of the Potomac."

"Boy, time tells the truth about all things."

"Yes, sir."

"And no one ever practised deception who did not get found out at last."

"No, sir: my folks taught me that. Sir, I am not practising any deception. I am telling you the truth."

"Boy, thee listen. I pity thy mother. How did thee cross the Potomac? Now see how soon thy story is brought to naught! The bridge over the Potomac was washed away or its middle part was broken down by the freshet. One of our men came from there only two days ago."

"There!" said excited Nance, "yees sin ha' found ye out already. Go 'long! Com' here frightening a poor woman like me, and all dese chillerns——"

"Nance, I am talking," said the old Quaker. "Boy, answer me: how did you cross the Potomac?"

"The horse walked on the water, sir!"

"Hebbens and earth, hear that!" said Black Nance, bowing down again. "I wonder dem forty she-bears dat dey read about in de Scripters don't com' out o' de woods and 'wower you up. Walked on de water, like de chariots o' de 'Risralites. Did I ebber hear a boy lie like dat now? I nebber did."

The old man sat silent. He at last shook his snuff-box again. "George Fairfax," he at last said slowly, "do thee keep thine eye on *that* boy."

"He'll be dead ripe, sure, by hanging-time," added Black Nance. "You come 'way from 'im, now, quick!" she called to one of her children whom she thought was dangerously near Harry. "You don't know what may happen to a boy like dat. De race o' Ann'ias and Sopiry wot de preacher tell about are not all dun gone yet, sure."

"Harry Mendell," continued the Quaker, "*is* that thy name?"

"Yes, sir."

"Thy story is improbable."

"It is true, sir."

"Heaven forbid that I should judge any one, even a boy. Harry Mendell, didst thou not steal that horse?"

"Steal? I steal? I would die, sir, before I would steal or lie. My father is a poor man and my mother is touched in mind, but we are all *honest* people."

"Your mother is touched in mind. It may be that accounts for it." The old man from Philadelphia turned to Lord Fairfax, who now came leisurely walking along the veranda, a very giant. "A most extraordinary case this, my friend, most extraordinary."

The great lord bent his gray eyes on the boy.

An overseer named Loveland who had stood at one corner of the house assumed an officious air and said: "I will bring out a whip from the stables. A boy that is too smart in mind ought to have a *leetle* smartness applied to his body as a relief."

"Yar, yar!" cried old Nance and the little negroes.

Harry thought of his mother and burst into tears. He put up his arms and buried his face in them and sobbed aloud. His attitude touched the hearts of the spectators, even that of the great lord. There was a long silence, broken only by some squirrels running among the vines and the expressed sympathy of one poor dog, who seemed to have a sense of the scene, and resting upon his haunches threw up his head and gave a long, piteous howl.

Suddenly there was a sound of horse's hoofs. A splendid bay mare with a broken bridle came running around the corner of the house. She seemed excited and whinnied.

Harry thought of his mother and burst into tears.

Harry knew that voice, dropped his arms, and stood staring in astonishment at the beautiful but nervous animal named Gay that he called "Scatter-hoof." How fine and intelligent the animal looked! Where had she been for nearly two days?

"What does thee suppose she is thinking of?" asked the Quaker.

She held her head high in the air, as if listening. There was a fiery brightness in her eye, and one could see her veins swell and muscles quiver. She pawed the turf with one foot impatiently and whinnied again.

Harry went up to her. She did not shrink from him. Her whole attitude seemed to say: "You can help me! Why will you not do it?"

The Quaker glanced down at her broken foot. "Boy, art thou sure that thee treated that horse well in thy drive when thou wert out of sight?"

Harry turned with an air of injured self-respect.

"Sir, I never treated this animal when I was out of sight from what I would have done in the view of anybody. I am a poor boy and a friendless one, but there is nothing in my life that I would not be willing to have everybody know!"

"And yet thou saidst that that horse walked across the Potomac River on the water."

"Sir, to my own harm I said it. I told my story

wholly as it seemed to me. I knew that it would injure me. I knew that you would not believe me! I told it just as it seemed to me, because it was the truth, and whatever may happen I will be true to my true self—always."

CHAPTER IV.

A MYSTERY.

OLD Lord Fairfax and his Quaker friend, whose name was Burns, were seated side by side on the long and famous veranda of Greenway Court when the strange horse appeared. George Washington, the young and accurate surveyor, and George William Fairfax, the young cousin of the old forest lord, had taken seats beside them. An Indian chieftain, called the Half-King, had come to the Court with a few of his followers, and the Indians had followed the strange horse as she had run around the yards near the stables.

It was a picturesque group: the proud old English baron, the wise Quaker, the two Georges, the Indians, the negroes, and the friendless, crying, yet resolute boy. After a night storm the autumn sun blazed in the clear, still blue sky, and the day was like a golden treasury—one of the beautiful days in the forests of the Shenandoah.

"Whoa!" shouted the old lord, in a voice of decision, as soon as the mare appeared.

"She is lame, friend Fairfax," said the Quaker before reproving Harry "See there, a shoe has come off and her hoof is broken. Dost thou see? A part of her hoof must have come off with her shoe."

"Collie shod that horse," said the overseer. "I can see his marks on the heel side of the shoes. The boy must have ridden her hard over the rocks. It is not often that a shoe is torn off like that. Boy, it is no use for you to whimper—you stole that horse and drove her down the rocks. You ought to be sent to jail. Confess now, or I will flog you till you run with blood! You know what I say is true. Now confess!"

The overseer raised a long, sinewy whip, cracked it twice in the air, and seized the boy by the arm, saying, "Now, sir, confess!"

"Wait a minute, my friend," said the Quaker. "Don't let us be hasty in our judgments. Let us question the boy a little further."

"You may do the questioning," said Lord Fairfax, "and I will act as judge. These things happened on my premises, I believe."

"Boy, thee must be honest now. We are all honest men here, and we desire to do only what is just right. Look up!" The old Quaker pounded with his cane. "Thee sayest that this horse was frightened by the Indians at the horse market on the Potomac?"

"Yes, sir, I speak the truth. The horse was frightened by the Indians who broke into the camp."

"I hope that thee does speak the truth as thou sayest, my lad. Thee looks honest, and the tone of thy speech rings honest, but what thou sayest does not seem likely or reasonable. Yet stranger things have been true. Friend Fairfax, what thinkest thou?"

"The boy's story is not likely or reasonable, friend Burns, but on that one point it might be true."

The negroes grinned at the boy, and seemed exultant that the case appeared against him.

"Boy, listen: be true to your conscience now. No man can lie and not be found out some time. Truth is her own vindicator. All the universe contradicts a liar. Truth is sure to be revealed in the end——"

"Then. one day, sir, I shall be seen to be honest," said the boy. "I am telling the truth sir, if it be to my own hurt."

"But you have not been telling the truth," said the overseer. "You said that the horse walked over the Potomac on the water."

"Slowly, slowly," said the Quaker. "Boy, be careful now. To whom does the horse belong?"

"To Squire Lawrence, of Winchester among the Hills."

"The young lawyer?"

"Yes, sir."

4

" Your master?"

" We live on his premises. We are sick and poor—
I mean my father and mother, sir. My father is a
cripple, sir, and my mother is not like other folks;
she is not well in mind, sir; out of her head at times,
sir."

" The mare has lately been separated from her
colt?" asked the Quaker.

" Yes, sir."

" And the colt was raised with the mare in Winchester?"

" Yes, sir."

" Thou sayest the animal was headstrong and ran
toward the south and crossed the Potomac and came
in this direction because thee couldst not curb her.
Boy, dost thee not see that thy story is unlikely?"

" Yes, sir."

" Then why does thee tell it?"

" Because, sir, it is true."

" Friend Fairfax, what does thee think of that
point?"

" A wholly unlikely story. The mare would have
run in the direction of her old home and foal. A
horse's instincts are as keen as a dog's. Drop the rein
anywhere, and a mare will turn toward home if she
have a colt."

" Yas, yas," shouted the negroes in a chorus.

"Boy, thy looks and tones seem true, but thy speech is against thee. Listen to me again. I wish to help thee. Thou sayest that the horse crossed the Potomac walking on the water. Dost thee not know that that were impossible?"

"I know it seems so, sir."

"Then why dost thou make such statements, boy?"

"Because they seem to me to be true, sir. If I make my case better in your eyes now by lying, I would have sin on my soul and time would find me out. How would I feel then? You would think me true but I would know myself to be false."

"Thou dreamedst that thee crossed the river on the water, lad. How about that?"

"No, sir, I did not dream. I was wide awake, sir."

"Thy head may be out of order like thy mother's, lad. I would wish that it were so."

"I cannot say. I think my head is as clear as others', sir, and I know that my soul is free from any false speaking, sir."

"Tut, tut!" said the puzzled Quaker, pounding his cane in his usual manner, "this is very extraordinary—very extraordinary."

"*Cunjured,*" said Black Nance, shaking her turban, "cunjured, sure. I can tell."

"Friend Fairfax, what does thee think of these suggestions?"

"I think that the boy's story in regard to the horse being frightened by the Indians is unlikely; that his statement that the animal became heady and ran south, when her home and her colt were to the northward in Winchester, is wholly improbable; and that his claim that she crossed the Potomac without ferry-boat or bridge is impossible. On this last point the boy is certainly untruthful, and as we *know—know*, I say—him to be untruthful on one point, we may reasonably think him so on all. I want to be charitable to the boy; he looks and acts honest, but his story cannot be true."

The negroes cried again in chorus, "Yas, yas!" Nance bowed her head and said, "I telt ye so." The very jays in the trees seemed mocking the boy and the dogs eyed him suspiciously.

There was a long silence. Then Lord Fairfax said: "Well, friend Burns, what would you say ought to be done in a case like this?"

"The case seems to be against him, but, friend Fairfax, I can discern spirits, and as sure as the heavens are true to us all at last, that boy believes what he says. He *thinks* that he speaks the truth."

"If I give him over to you," said the old lord to the overseer, "what will you do with him?"

"Flog him, the cunning canting rascal, and put him to work. He's a slick one. He knows that he never crossed the Potomac on the water in a flood. He swam the horse across."

"Then he must be witless not to have stated it so. I cannot see his motive in making so foolish a statement against himself."

"I tell ye his hoss wer' *cunjured*," said old Nance. "I com' from Guinea, I did, an' I know when folks are cunjured. I can discern things, too."

"Shut up, you black witch," said the overseer.

"Yas, sir," said the negress, shrinking away, "but I knows; ole Nance knows."

The overseer seized the boy angrily and lifted his whip again, saying, "Now, sir!" The boy's eyes stood out, and his face was white and his little frame quivered. He looked up to the blue sky. "God help me!" he said helplessly.

A man on horseback rode up.

"A fine morning. You are welcome, Reuben Rouzé."

"A fine morning, indeed." He started. "What has brought that boy here? He was at the fair when the Indians surprised us."

There was a deep silence. "Then—there—were—Indians—and—they—did—surprise—you?" said the Quaker in measured tones.

"Yes."

"This is all very extraordinary," said the Quaker,

turning to Lord Fairfax; "one of the boy's stories is true."

"But he stole the horse," said the overseer, "and lied in regard to his crossing the Potomac on the water. That last point is clear enough to any one."

"Overseer," said the old lord, "take the boy, but do not strike him a blow till I give the order."

Reuben Rouzé was a popular man on the Northern Neck, but he was land-poor. He had a comfortable but plain home, a good wife, and a family of children. He had a great heart whose charity never failed, and all the persons of the Northern Neck, from the great Lord Fairfax to the poorest negro, felt that he had a true friend in Reuben Rouzé.

"Mr. Rouzé," said Lord Fairfax, "that boy has been telling us a strange story. He said that your camp over the Potomac was surprised by the Indians. That you say was true."

"My Lord Fairfax, that was true."

"And that he was told to secure that horse, which had been frightened by the Indians and seems to have been running away."

"My Lord Fairfax, that is true. I heard the order. I was about to tell the men the old story of 'The Jolly Harper Man,' when a war-whoop pierced the air. The very animals were stricken with terror. *That* mare broke her tether and ran into the woods toward the south."

"Dost thou hear that, friend Fairfax?" asked the Quaker. "She was alarmed by the Indians and ran south. We doubted that part of the boy's story when we first heard it. Let us be very slow in our judgments now, very charitable now, friend Fairfax. Stranger things than that story have been true."

"What should have made the mare run *south?*" asked Lord Fairfax.

"I do not know. She may—she may—now it occurs to me—she may have left her colt somewhere in that direction. That would have been something like the story of 'The Jolly Harper Man.'"

"No—she belongs to Winchester. But what is the story of 'The Jolly Harper Man?'"

"Oh, an old Scotch ballad tale of the Border—a minstrel story. I will recite the ballad to you some evening. It's a queer story of a mare that was separated from her colt, and did queer things and made a queer run."

"I like those old stories," said the lord. "I never heard of that one before."

"How did the boy get here?" asked Mr. Rouzé. "The river is flooded below the upper fords, the bridge is gone, and there is no ferry."

"That is the remarkable thing we have been discussing and cannot find out. He says that the horse ran away and walked over the river *on the water*, or seemed to him to walk on the water. It is impossible to believe that a mare with a colt at Winchester would run away to the south and cross the Potomac without a bridge."

"She may have run away and *swam* across the river," said Mr. Rouzé. "Things like that have happened."

"That would make the boy's story seem a little more probable. But the boy persistently denies that she swam across."

"The boy is a thief," said the overseer, "and attempted to steal the horse. He swam her across the river and made up the story that he told. It is a mere waste of breath to talk more about it."

The overseer tossed his head contemptuously and impudently.

"I cannot think that the boy is a thief," said Mr. Rouzé. "Let me see him."

"You believe in everybody," said the overseer. "You are every man's friend."

"It helps people to believe in them," said Mr. Rouzé. "Faith in people makes them grow."

"And keeps them from hanging," said the overseer, with a sneer.

"Well," said the Quaker, "charity never faileth!

Go talk with the boy. They say in these parts that you are a true-hearted man, and to be believed to be true-hearted is the greatest honor any man can have in this world."

Rouzé sought Harry. He held with him a long conversation. It ended with this strange dialogue:

"Harry," said Mr. Rouzé, "I love you and believe in you. But you are deceived. You did not attempt to steal the mare. She thought that her colt was at some place in the direction she went. She was heady. That is my theory. But she did not walk over the river on the water. She swam, and you were frightened and deceived. No, Harry, only come with me and say to Lord Fairfax that you were deceived, and I can secure your release and send you home."

"But she did *not* swim. She stood on the water, or so it seemed to me."

"Harry"—Mr. Rouzé was a tender-hearted and loving man. He put his arm around the boy and drew him to his side.

The boy burst into tears. He felt that the man was his friend: he loved him. Two hearts were certainly true to him, his mother's and this good planter's.

"I think," said Mr. Rouzé, "that Washington believes in you. He is the soul of honor and of truth. Confess this one error and I will send you home."

"Mr. Rouzé, I would do anything for you. But the thing happened just as I have said. I would not wish to be sent home with a stain on my character. O Mr. Rouzé, everybody believes in you. Take me home with you and believe in me, and one day you will find that my soul is as honest and true and as faithful as the Georges'."

"Not now," said Mr. Rouzé.

"Then I will be left to the overseer."

CHAPTER V.

AN ACHING HEART.

THE first question that Harry Mendell asked of the overseer was if he could go to his home in North Winchester to see his father and mother. "I will return," said he.

"You are a prisoner," said the overseer, "and are only allowed to remain at large by the good will of the lord. You must remain here or be arrested. People who can ride on the air and walk on the water need a careful eye kept on them."

"But, sir, why should I be a prisoner? What have I done that is wrong? Of what am I accused?"

"Of theft, thief."

"But, sir, I did not steal the bay mare. I was ordered to find her and not to leave her; and she forced me to come this way."

"You attempted to steal her and lied to cover up your wrong."

"But what could have been my motive? I never tried to put the horse to my own use in any way or to sell her."

47

"There is some mystery about the whole matter, and you will be detained here until it is cleared up. Had you fallen into other hands you would have been sent to jail. Boy, do you think that the people of Greenway Court are fools? You young rascal! I can hardly keep my hands off you when I think of that foolish story you told! Would *you* yourself believe that a horse crossed the flooded Potomac *on the water* if *I* had said so?"

"No, sir, I would not. But I told the story just as it appeared to me. I could not tell it otherwise. My mother is poor, and sometimes she is out of her mind, but she is an *honest* woman; we are an honest family, as I have said. Oh, my poor old mother! Her mind would go out entirely if she were to hear of this. I pity her all the time. A prisoner! Harry Mendell a prisoner! And the disgrace of the suspicion will hang over me for life."

He looked up to the sky. A cloud was passing. He dropped his eyes, saying, "Would that my trouble were like that! Maybe mine may never pass! How can I ever prove that what I say is true?"

"If what you said were true, time would prove it. But time does not prove what is impossible," said the overseer.

A day or two after the strange event the horse was sent home to Winchester among the Hills.

"Now mother will know all," he said. "But her heart will never doubt me," he thought, comforting himself with a more hopeful view. "She will ever be true to me—my poor old mother! I think that the Georges believe me. Mr. Rouzé does, I know."

He cried again as he saw the horse carried away, and begged to be allowed to accompany it, promising again to return.

"No," said the overseer; "you are the most stubborn baby that I ever met."

A week passed. He was set to work with the surveyors. He followed the two Georges, carrying a surveyor's chain and tools. The two young men treated him kindly, and never alluded in his presence to the crime of which he was accused.

Once, by the camp-fire, as he was sitting thinking, he burst into tears again. Both Georges were touched at the sight and spoke to him considerately.

"You do pity me?" he said in a helpless way. "But why should I ask any one's pity? I have only told everything just as it seemed to me to be true. A poor man has no hope except in a heart that is really good—like Mr. Rouzé's."

One evening as the young surveyors had returned to Greenway Court and the servants were stabling their horses, a strange and pitiful thing happened. The warm days of middle autumn had come into the

season like a parting visit of summer.   It was near
night, and the woods brought the sunset light so near
that the sun itself seemed going down just behind
the trees.

What was that?

A little old woman was standing among the trees
across the road, as if watching.   She had on a thin
shawl, a calash bonnet, and a scant dress, and leaned
upon a cane.   Her hair was white and fell about her
face.   Harry did not see her as soon as the light-
hearted, merry people on the great veranda.   But as
often as he came out of the stables she would approach the roadside and beckon, and call in a scared,
earnest voice, "Harry! Harry!" with a mysterious
wave of her thin white hand.

He saw her at last and stood speechless.   He then
glanced toward the people on the veranda and said:
"That is my mother!"

He put down a pail that he was carrying and ran
across the road to meet her.

"Oh, mother, why have you come?   Do you know
it all?"

"Yes, all—all—that is why I have come.   I've
come to comfort ye.   They won't take ye to jail, will
they, Harry?"

"No, mother, I hope not."

"Don't ye worry if they do.   A mother's heart

doesn't fail at jails, Harry—nor in death, Harry—nor anywhere, Harry. I know that every word that ye have spoken is true. Oh, my boy, my boy, God pity the poor—I've nothing but these empty hands, Harry. Yes, I have. I own the heavens and I own the earth, and if I have no advocate here I have one in a better world than this! Harry, be true to the best that is in ye and trust God. He's tedious but he's sure."

He saw that she was growing excited. Her eyes had a strange, vacant, uncertain look. He heard the people laughing and repeating: "He's *tedious* but he's sure."

"Go, mother. I am sorry that I cannot offer you so much as a meal or a bed."

"I want no food. As for houses—trouble dwells in houses. I am going back, Harry. I will walk all night. My head aches, and I can feel my brain burn and beat. I only came to say to you that I know you to be true. I had to come. Unseen hands pushed me. They do sometimes!"

She turned and walked past the house, and then in full view of the veranda she threw back her calash, revealing her white hair.

The negroes looked at her with fear and wonder; the dogs circled doubtfully about her. As she moved back she stumbled and fell.

"Poor old woman," exclaimed a voice.

The people of the place ran toward her and offered her help, food, and lodgings. She refused all.

"I want nothing," she said.

"Go into the house," said they.

"Trouble dwells in houses," she repeated. "No, the out-of-doors house is my home. Harry's word's all I care for now. Only that, then let me die, no matter where. It's little matter what becomes of a poor old woman like me."

They offered to send her home in a carriage, but she refused any assistance.

"Let me cool my head in the air of the night. The roof of the sky is for all. Let a poor old woman go. My boy will be vindicated at last. Let me go, weak as I am." She looked back and said: "My heart and strength faileth, but God is the strength of my heart and my portion forever."

She stopped once more.

"Harry!"

And again: she called—

"Harry!"

"What, mother?"

"You stay where you are till you are vindicated. Honor is more than anything else: a good character is everything. Stay. God can wait. I can." She hobbled away, looking behind wistfully at times.

The people did not fully understand the scene. They stood around in pitying silence.

The boy took up the pail and went about his work. He ate no supper that evening; he wanted none. He disappeared. They found him late in the evening, asleep, his head resting on his arm, among the stacks of hay.

CHAPTER VI.

HIS MAJESTY'S JUSTICE OF THE PEACE.

ON a late autumn day when the afternoons were yet warm even while the winds brought storms of leaves to the forest, his majesty's justice of the peace rode up to Greenway Court and sat down beside Lord Fairfax, who was enjoying his pipe on the veranda.

"I have ridden over to talk with you about that stolen horse, my lord. You hold the boy, I hear."

"Yes—yes, sir," said Lord Fairfax. "There is no clear proof against him, and my Quaker visitor suggested that in such a case one should hesitate before using the law. Has the owner of the horse made any complaint?"

"No. I saw Esquire Lawrence at Northern Winchester. He told me the story of the horse and the boy's story as you conveyed it to him with the horse by one of your grooms. Mr. Lawrence says that the story may be true except in the part of the manner of crossing the river. The colt was sold to a man in

Fredericksburg, and the mare and colt were brought down from the Northern hills and were separated in the road near Greenway Court. So the mare may have thought that the colt was here."

Lord Fairfax shook his pipe. The fine manly form of George Washington appeared on the veranda, and the young surveyor seemed to listen to the last statement with peculiar interest.

"That is very strange," said Lord Fairfax, "and it makes probable another part of the boy's story that at first seemed improbable. Were it not for the incident of the manner of crossing the Potomac, I should believe the boy to be honest. What do you think, Master George?"

"I believe that the boy is honest in all that he said, but somehow is deceived in his opinion of the manner that the horse crossed the Potomac. I think that he shows the right spirit even in the story which he knows he is telling to his own harm. I would not do or say anything that could possibly shield a young horse-thief, but that boy has not the look of a thief or a liar. I would be sorry to see harm come to him. Sincerity has its own air, and it cannot be counterfeited. The boy's grief seems to be because his honor is questioned. I believe in the boy and pity him, and I am slow and watchful in forming my opinions."

Lord Fairfax sent a servant for one of his grooms, who soon appeared before the veranda.

"I want you to ride over to Northern Winchester," he said, "and to inquire *where* the mare of Esquire Lawrence was separated from her colt."

"You take great pains, my lord, to protect the honor of a poor boy," said the esquire.

"Honor," said young Washington, "is everything, and it ought to be as sacred to a poor boy as a rich boy, and in this case it seems to be so. I am glad that the groom is to be sent."

"May it please my master," said the groom, "I already know where the mare was separated from her colt. Squire Lawrence's hostler rode down to the Court here on the mare followed by her colt, along with the man who had purchased the colt. The hostler wished to see me. The purchaser of the colt was named Adler—John Adler. Squire Lawrence's groom returned with the bay mare, and I kept the colt in the great meadow stable over night, and Mr. Adler stayed with me over night in my cabin, and took the colt with his own horse to Fredericksburg the next day."

"Then the colt stopped at the stables here over night?" asked the esquire.

"Yes, your honor, about a mile from here."

"But why did you not tell us that before?"

"I did not know that it would serve your honor.   I had nothing to conceal.   I thought my conduct was right, your honor.   The strange horse was around the meadow stables for a day."

"So it seems that the colt was stabled on these very premises," said Lord Fairfax slowly.

"But surely my Lord Fairfax does not think that the mare had such a *knowledge of geography as that*.   If so, she would make a good surveyor.   George, here, with all his accuracy, could hardly have a better knowledge of the compass."

"I do not know, I do not know," said Lord Fairfax. "They say that the mother's instinct in animals is a very wonderful thing."

"I get the trend of your thoughts," said his majesty's justice.   "You half suspect that the mare ran away against her bridle and forced her way here, and that that brought the boy here, and that it was a sense of honor that compelled the boy to stick to her until they came to the surveyors' camp. Were such a thing true it would be extraordinary."

At this point of the conversation Mr. Rouzé rode up before the veranda and dismounted.   He was on his way to Fredericksburg.   Harry saw him from his work in the tobacco sheds, and, knowing the man's generous and friendly heart, drew near to the veranda.   Mr. Rouzé recognized him with an encouraging, "Well, my boy," and Harry's heart warmed with sympathy.

"Been talking about that strange affair of the boy and the horse," said the justice to Mr. Rouzé. "What is your opinion about it, now—ought the boy to be arrested?"

"Arrested! No! He has told what he believes to be true from the first. As for the horse—well, I have been over to Lawrence's. It is a case like the old Scotch story of 'The Jolly Harper Man,' that I began to tell at the horse fair when the Indians set the trees to whooping all around us. What a day that was!"

"What is your story of 'The Jolly Harper Man?'" asked Lord Fairfax. "Give your horse to the groom and have some supper with us. Take a pipe and tell us all the story."

"Excuse me until Christmas night, your lordship. I must go home to my family now."

"You all seem to be weakening in regard to this case," said the sheriff.

Mr. Rouzé looked at Harry. "Boy, I have seen your old mother. I pity her. She thinks a deal of you."

The tears gathered again in Harry's eyes.

"Boy, she wants that I should take you. I would be glad to, but I have more mouths than I can feed now."

"I wish you would roof the boy," said Lord Fairfax.

"Something may be in him for aught I know—and it is my nature to give every one a chance, and sometimes a second chance."

"Your lordship, I want to do it, but I am poor."

"Yes, but you have a great heart; about the biggest heart in all Virginia. You ought to have been rich. No man that I know would make a better use of his money. Have you heard that that mare and her colt were separated on these premises?"

"Yes, I heard so at Squire Lawrence's."

"I am of the opinion that you and I are thinking of the same thing. But that does not prove anything. The boy knows that that horse did not fly or walk on the water. But so many things that he told at first, that I did not believe, have proved true or reasonable that I am willing to suspend judgment, if the justice here so advises, and I am sure he will take my view: he is a just man."

The sheriff felt the compliment. "I am persuaded that your lordship is prudent," said he.

"Mr. Rouzé," said Lord Fairfax, "the overseer is disposed to be hard on the boy. I wish that you would take him to your own home, seeing that his folks are poor and there is some mystery about the case, and nothing seems to have been said to the boy's discredit before. A gentleman of honor would not ruin a poor boy. Give him a chance—give him a chance; and if ever you get into trouble we'll re-member you favorably, won't we, George?"

George Washington turned an eye of kindly ad-miration upon the good-hearted, chivalrous old man.

"Boy," said Mr. Rouzé, "do you wish to go with me?"

Harry's face beamed. "Yes, sir."

"Well, jump up here."

Harry leaped into the saddle before Mr. Rouzé and settled back on the man's bosom. Mr. Rouzé put one arm around the boy, shook the reins with the other hand, and bowing to Lord Fairfax, the sheriff, and young George Washington, rode away.

CHAPTER VII.

REUBEN ROUZÉ.

A S Harry felt the friendliness of Mr. Rouzé's arm around his shoulder, his feelings gave way, and he was resolved to tell the kindly man all his heart. So as the two rode along toward Fredericksburg, in the shadows of the great forest of the Northern Neck, he said:

"Mr. Rouzé, I am a poor boy, and I have no friend but you and my sick father, and you know how it is with mother."

"Yes, yes—you are having a hard time, and I am sorry for you, and I am going to do all for you I can. You have one friend besides me and your folks, Harry. Every one has who is honest."

"Who—Washington?"

"No—Time."

"Yes, Mr. Rouzé, but it takes so long."

"I know that Washington is your friend. I heard him say that somehow he believed that your story seemed to you to be true. Listen, my boy! Is there not some way that we might prove your story to be true? If we could, the people at Greenway Court would take an especial interest in you and might help you. They are high-born people; and old Lord Fairfax and young George Washington like a man of honor. If you could prove your story, they would both become your friends and might help you. Now listen and think—have you told me *all?*"

"Mr. Rouzé, I have told you the truth to the best of my recollection. There is one thing that lately has seemed to me more strange than the rest. When the horse *seemed floating* across the river that dark night, I thought that I heard her feet strike a spike. That sound haunts me. I can hear it still."

"'Seemed floating,' you said. Was that the way it seemed?"

"Yes, Mr. Rouzé."

"Harry, my boy, you were dreaming!"

"No, Mr. Rouzé, I was as wide awake as now."

"But, my boy, when the moon came out and you looked down, what did you see?"

"Water."

"You looked down into the water?"

"Yes."

"Did you see any log or spike?"

"No."

"It is very strange. Now, Harry, you are not lying, are you?"

"Mr. Rouzé, how could I lie to a man like you? I love you more than the whole world, except poor father and mother. I would die for you, Mr. Rouzé!"

Mr. Rouzé drew him close to him in silence.

"I would die for you, Mr. Rouzé," Harry repeated. There was a long silence. They heard the falling leaves and saw the glimmering of the sunbeams slanting amid the trees.

"Mr. Rouzé, you said that Time would be my friend. Do you believe in God?"

"Yes, Harry."

"Time will repay you for all you do for me. God will. Mr. Rouzé, *I will!*"

They stopped by a running brook amid flaming maples. Harry loosened the reins and the horse stopped to drink. The great woods were bright with yellow leaves and sunbeams. There was an earthy odor about the brook and the whir of partridge-wings now and then in the air. As they sat waiting for the horse to drink, Harry turned to his benefactor and looked him clearly in the eye.

"Mr. Rouzé, there come times in life when every one needs a friend."

"Yes."

"You may, some day."

"Likely, my boy."

"I will be true to you then. You will remember what I have said to you here by the brook. No matter what may happen, Mr. Rouzé, I will be as true to you then as you have been to me."

"Harry, to own *one* true heart is a possession more than gold. That man is the richest of all who has true-hearted friends. I like to read the parable of the steward in the Testament. Some people don't like that. I think that the wisdom of the world is in it. Harry, I am poor. I am one of the poorest land-holders in all Virginia. I live in a log cabin—I have not the money to build so much as a good house. Young Washington once said that he would help me when he should be older and his estates were settled. He is a man of few words, but he seems to have a kindly feeling toward me."

"Mr. Rouzé, I know how to work. It would make me happy to work for you. I will be as faithful to you as though you were my own father."

An old negro passed them on the way, with a bundle on a stick over his shoulder. He clapped off his hat with an odd wave of his hand.

"Where are you going, Pete?" asked Mr. Rouzé.

"I's been sent for," was the reply.

Harry started.

"Mr. Rouzé, I have something more to tell. I met a negro on the night that the mare ran away, and he said those very words, 'I's been sent for,' or like them. He tried to turn the mare, but she wouldn't go that way. Mr. Rouzé, if we could only find him, you would believe him. I met him close to the bank of the river, where the mare went over." There was a thoughtful silence.

"Oh, Mr. Rouzé, if I could only have my good name back again! I am helpless—won't you go with me some day and try to find the negro that I met that night? The people at Greenway Court would believe you. You would believe the negro. Oh, how I wish it might be so!"

"It is a long distance, Harry. I shall be going that way some day, and I will take you with me."

"Oh, if you only would! Mr. Rouzé, think of my mother. I think of her all the time. My good name was all that was left to give her pride and comfort, and now that is gone; she would die for me, as I would for you. Her heart is true in every beat, and she can't help her 'spells.' Oh, how I have seen her struggle against them!"

They came to a house with two chimneys and a slanting roof. It was near Fredericksburg.

"The mother of Washington lives there," said Mr. Rouzé. "She is a noble woman. She manages the estate. We will stop at the door and I will tell her that George is well."

"Is this the place where Washington threw the stone across the river?" asked Harry.

"Yes," said Mr. Rouzé.

The plantation was on the Rappahannock, opposite the town. It was called "Pine Grove," from a body of great trees near the house. The negroes sometimes called it the "Ferry Farm." Here Augustine Washington, the father of George Washington, died, on "ye 12th day of April, 1743, aged 49 years," from a congestion caused by riding over his plantation in a cold storm. George Washington was eleven years of age at the time of his father's death.

After the death of her husband, Mary Washington gave her life to the care of her family, with the devotion of a great heart and mind. Her step-son, Lawrence Washington, was her adviser. The plantation raised wool, flax, tobacco, and corn; carding and spinning wool were carried on in the house. Spinning-wheels buzzed in the busy rooms, which looked out on great fields and gardens. The Rappahannock flowed in full view, and the family at Pine Grove were happy and prosperous.

Here George Washington passed his early years, at times visiting his half-brother, Lawrence, who married, in the year after his father's death, Annie Fairfax, the daughter of Hon. William Fairfax, of Belvoir, an elegant estate adjoining Mount Vernon, which later became George Washington's own home.

The estates of Belvoir, Mount Vernon, and the landed aristocracy of Virginia were very large, and Greenway Court surpassed them all in size, as it was intended that it should do some day in the grandeur of its manor-house. The home of Mary Washington was humble, but most of the houses of the Virginian planters were large, elegant, and richly furnished.

Mr. John Esten Cooke, who once lived amid the associations of these ancient estates, thus speaks of their stately provincial life at the time of the Washingtons, the Fairfaxes, and the Lees, in his "Golden Age of Virginia:"

"Care seemed to keep away from it and stand out of its sunshine. The planter in his manor-house, surrounded by his family and retainers, was a feudal patriarch, mildly ruling everybody. He drank wholesome wine, sherry or canary, of his own importation; entertained every one; held great festivities at Christmas, with huge log-fires in the great fireplaces around which the family clan gathered; and everybody, high and low, seemed to be happy. It was the life of the family, not of the great world, and produced that intense attachment for the soil which has become proverbial; which made a Virginian once say,

'If I had to leave Virginia, I would not know where to go.'

"Such luxuries as were desired, books, wines, silks, and laces, were brought from London to the planter's wharf in exchange for his tobacco; and he was content to pay well for all if he could thereby escape living in towns."

Harry was now amid the scenes of George Washington's childhood. He talked with Mr. Rouzé about the incidents of his silent friend's early life. Mr. Rouzé merely knew that Washington as a boy was noted for sense and honor.

"He will be heard of some day," he said. "Genius is born young. He is a man in prudence already, and the times are going to need such as he."

A number of stories used to be related of Washington's boyhood, and as it is our purpose to picture his early life incidentally in this story, we may speak of them here. They are curious from their simplicity, and were for the most part collected by Rev. Mr. Weems, a minister of one of the parishes in which Washington lived, from neighborhood traditions. The story of the "little hatchet" was at one period a moral tale which was told with great interest by New England firesides, but which too much repetition came to give a humorous coloring.

We must give the reader the popular version of

some of these old stories which Mr. Weems collected from local sources. They are well known, but the reader will like to see them as they used to be told, now that we have come to visit Washington's early home.

The famous story of George and the hatchet in its original simplicity ran as follows:

"When George was about six years old he was made the wealthy master of a hatchet; of which, like most little boys, he was immoderately fond, and was constantly going about chopping everything that came in his way. One day, in the garden, where he often amused himself hacking his mother's pea-sticks, he unluckily tried the edge of his hatchet on the body of a beautiful young English cherry-tree, which he barked so terribly that I don't believe the tree ever got the better of it. The next morning the old gentleman, finding out what had befallen his tree, which, by the by, was a great favorite, came into the house, and with much warmth asked for the mischievous author, declaring at the same time that he would not have taken five guineas for his tree. Nobody could tell him anything about it. Presently George and his hatchet made their appearance. 'George,' said his father, 'do you know who killed that beautiful little cherry-tree yonder in the garden?' This was a tough question, and George staggered under it for

6

a moment, but quickly recovered himself; and looking at his father with the sweet face of youth brightened with the inexpressible charm of all-conquering
truth, he bravely cried out: 'I can't tell a lie, pa;
you know I can't tell a lie. I did cut it with my
hatchet.' 'Run to my arms, you dearest boy!'
cried his father in transports; 'run to my arms; glad
am I, George, that you killed my tree; for you have
paid me for it a thousand-fold. Such an act of heroism in my son is of more worth than a thousand trees,
though blossomed with silver and their fruits of
purest gold.' "

This sounds rather oriental, but the lesson is good.

Another story of like import once popular took this
form:

"The mother of Washington had purchased a pair
of beautiful gray horses, and was accustomed to turn
them to pasture in a meadow in front of the house,
from whence she could see them while sitting at
the window. At one time she owned a favorite
young colt which had never been broken to the
saddle and which no one was permitted to ride.
One day, while several young lads were at the
house on a visit, they proposed after dinner to
mount the colt and make the circuit of the pasture.
They attempted to mount, but were defeated. Washington, however, succeeded, and gave the favorite

such a race that he at length fell under his rider.
He immediately went and told his mother what he
had done; she said to him, 'I forgive you, George,
because you have the courage to tell the truth.' "

The following true incident of the scenes of Washington's home life is well told in Sparks' "Life of
Washington:"

"Washington's eldest brother Lawrence had been
an officer in the late war, and served at the siege of
Carthagena and in the West Indies. Being a well-
informed and accomplished gentleman, he had acquired the esteem and confidence of General Went-
worth and Admiral Vernon, the commanders of the
expedition, with whom he afterward kept up a friendly
correspondence. Having observed the military turn
of his young brother, and looking upon the British
navy as the most direct road to distinction in that
line, he obtained for George a midshipman's warrant,
in the year 1746, when he was fourteen years old.
This step was taken with an authority to which nature
gave a claim.

"At this critical juncture, Mr. Jackson, a friend of
the family, wrote to Lawrence Washington as follows:
'I am afraid Mrs. Washington will not keep up her
first resolution. She seems to dislike George's going
to sea, and says several persons have told her it was
a bad scheme. She offers several trifling objections,

such as fond unthinking mothers habitually suggest;
and I find that one word against his going has more
weight than ten for it.' She persisted in opposing the
plan, and it was given up. Nor ought that decision
to be ascribed to obstinacy or maternal weakness. It
was her eldest son, whose character and manners
must already have exhibited a promise full of solace
and hope to a widowed mother, on whom alone devolved the charge of four young children. To see
him separated from her at so tender an age, exposed
to the perils of accident and the world's rough usage,
without a parent's voice to counsel or a parent's
hand to guide, and to enter on a theatre of action
which would forever remove him from her presence,
was a trial of her fortitude and sense of duty which
she could not be expected to hazard without reluc-
tance and concern.

"Washington must certainly have cherished a great
regard for his mother, or he would not have ordered
his baggage to be returned home, which was already
put on board the vessel destined to convey him to
his new vocation as a midshipman, and entirely
abandon his cherished purpose to take part in the
war in which Great Britain was then engaged.
George remained at school, and some other boy
secured the midshipman's berth."

But we must return to our story.

It was near nightfall when Mr. Rouzé and Harry rode up to the door. The river rippled in the light winds, the great fields wore a brown haze, and the stacks and cribs indicated the closing year.

A company of slaves, led by curiosity, gathered around the callers, and some of them offered their services in caring for the horse and for the comforts of the travellers.

The door slowly opened, and a stately woman of some fifty or more years stood before them. She had a beautiful, benevolent face; she was neatly but plainly dressed, and a key-basket of stout wicker-work covered with leather hung by her side, out of which protruded the silver handles of a pair of scissors.

"You are welcome, Mr. Rouzé," said the lady. "Come in and rest and take tea with me, and let the groom care for your horse. Have you been travelling far?"

"I have come from Greenway Court, and stopped to wish you good health and to tell you that George is well."

"You are a good man, Mr. Rouzé, always thoughtful of the happiness of others. You seem to live in the happiness that you create, and I owe many good recollections to your thoughtful favors. I hope that if you ever should want friends, the world will be as mindful of you as you are of others. You will please me if you stop and rest."

"I would be glad to please you, madam, but I must reach home to-night."

"What boy is that you have, Mr. Rouzé?"

"His name is Harry Mendell. His folks are sick and he is friendless."

"He will find a friend in you. But, Mr. Rouzé, I am a very plain-spoken woman. Are you able to do all these things that you are doing for every one in need? Let me help you if you have a good case, Mr. Rouzé."

"You are very kind, madam, but this is a peculiar case. The boy knows George, and you may meet him again."

Mr. Rouzé bowed, Harry uncovered his head, and the two rode away.

There was a place on the Rappahannock, near Fredericksburg, where Washington had thrown a stone to the opposite bank of the river. As the feat was deemed an extraordinary one, many boys tried to equal it by throwing stones from the same place. But few young Virginians were successful—the stones fell short.

Harry Mendell during this brief visit to Washington's early home went out to throw a stone across the river. He attempted the feat again and again, but

failed.   But at last, by an impulse that concentrated
all his energy, he sent a stone across, greatly to the
delight of Mr. Rouzé.

"In one thing, at least, you are Washington's
equal," said the latter.   The incident was an inspiration to the boy.

The sun was going down.   The river was a sheet
of silvery light.   The air was still and the forests
flamed afar.

As they looked back they saw the smoke curling
above one of the two great chimneys and, with hands
shading her eyes, the courtly woman who had offered
them such kindly hospitality still watching them
from the door.   The fact that they "knew George"
had touched her heart, and her eyes lovingly followed
them until they were lost to sight.

The home of Mr. Rouzé was near Mount Vernon,
as the plantation came to be called which George
Washington received as his inheritance from his
father's estate, after the death of his half-brother,
Lawrence Washington.   The situation of the farm
was beautiful, on wooded hills.   The home was made
of logs and had been largely constructed by Mr.
Rouzé himself.   Mr. Rouzé was a young man, having a wife whose happiness it was to obey the law of
love in her own home.   The two Fairfaxes and the
two Washington families were near neighbors in

those times of immense distances.   It was some two
hundred miles from Williamsburg to Winchester, and
yet these with Fredericksburg and Alexandria were
neighboring towns.

The figures of Lawrence Washington and George
Washington were often seen in the picturesque forest
way that connected these four towns.   Lawrence
Washington fell into ill health, and went to Barba-
does, taking George, to whom he seems to have been
deeply attached.   He lived for a considerable period,
but never recovered his health.   After the death of
Lawrence Washington and the end of the French and
Indian War, George Washington spent some fifteen
years of peaceful life at Mount Vernon, and here he
brought his wife, Martha Custis, a beautiful widow
whom he married in 1759.

Such were the scenes of the boyhood of Washington.   His early days were spent among a simple,
sensible, true-hearted people.   He was schooled to
honor by his mother and the example of Lord Fairfax, and he had little education after his father died
that he did not himself acquire amid the Virginia
woods, valleys, and mountains.   Harry felt the force
of his character, and wished that he could have his
good name and grow into influence like him.   Could
this ever be?

CHAPTER VIII.

WASHINGTON'S ADVENTURES AS A SURVEYOR.

IT was a winter night. Lord Fairfax had gathered about him a merry company; Washington was there, but grave and reserved in contrast with the others. Mr. Gist, the explorer, was present, and with him had come young Owler, an Indian runner, to hear the violins. A number of young hunters and trappers and fur-traders had stopped at the Court for the night to share the bountiful baron's hospitality.

The stories of the surveys of his immense estates were Lord Fairfax's delight. Washington kept journals of his surveys, and Mr. Gist was a natural story-teller.

Owler, the Indian runner, sat by the great fire, and old Joe, Lord Fairfax's colored attendant, stood by his master at the side of the great oak table. There were instrumental music, singing of hunting songs, and story-telling.

After each story black Joe passed around a silver

snuff-box, and a part of the men, following a not un-common habit at that time, took pinches of snuff.

"Now," said Lord Fairfax, "let us listen to Wash-ington's journal of his surveys once more. I like to study that. It gives me a view of my own estates. Joe, you may pass the snuff-box, and don't forget our runner, Owler."

The men smiled. The idea of giving a young Indian runner a pinch of snuff amused them, and they were full of curiosity to see how the young run-ner would receive the offer of the explosive dust to which they were used. In passing the snuff-box they had neglected Owler.

Lord Fairfax spread the journal of young Wash-ington and its records of surveys out on the great oak table. He began to read the diary. The men listened eagerly, ready to applaud any incident of the narrative which should excite their interest. A Scotchman who acted as secretary to Lord Fairfax at times constantly said, "Hoot, men, that is good," and gave orders to black Joe in regard to the hospi-tality of the silver snuff-box.

Old Nance stood looking in the door from the hall, hoping to see Indian Owler take a pinch of snuff. She listened to the reading of the record intently, to see if it gave any account of "thunder weather." To her every tempest was like a judgment day.

The journal, except the record of surveys and un-
important matter, as read by Lord Fairfax was as follows:

JOURNAL

OF MY

JOURNEY OVER THE MOUNTAINS;

BY

GEORGE WASHINGTON,

WHILE SURVEYING FOR LORD THOMAS FAIRFAX,
BARON OF CAMERON,

IN THE

NORTHERN NECK OF VIRGINIA,

BEYOND THE BLUE RIDGE,

IN 1747-8.

"A Journal of my Journey over the Mountains
began Fryday the 11th of March 1747-8," began Lord
Fairfax, reading.   He paused after the introduction,
while his Scotch secretary put new logs on the fire.
He then continued reading:

"*Fryday March* 11th 1747-8.—Began my Journey in
Company with George Fairfax, Esqr.; we travell'd
this day 40 Miles to Mr George Neavels in Prince
William County."

"Forty miles," said the Scotchman.   "Hoot, men,
that were good now—that were good!"

"*Saturday March* 12th.—This Morning   Mr James

Genn ye surveyor came to us, we travel'd over ye Blue Ridge to Capt Ashbys on Shannandoah River. Nothing Remarkable happen'd.

"*Sunday March* 13th.—Rode to his Lordships Quarter about 4 Miles higher up y River   we went through most beautiful Groves of Sugar Trees & spent ye best part of y Day in admiring ye Trees & richness of ye Land.

"*Monday* 14th.—We sent our Baggage to Capt Hites (near Frederick Town) went ourselves down ye River about 16 Miles to Capt Isaac Penningtons (the Land exceeding Rich & Fertile all ye way produces abundance of Grain Hemp Tobacco &c) in order to Lay of some Lands on Cates Marsh & Long Marsh."

So far the reading was dull, but it became presently more interesting, and old Nance was heard to whisper, "Now we gwine to have thunder weather."

"*Tuesday* 15th.—We set out early with Intent to Run round ye s^d Land but being taken in a Rain & it Increasing very fast obliged us to return, it clearing about one oClock & our time being too Precious to Loose we a second time ventured out & Worked hard till Night & then return'd to Penningtons we got our Suppers & was Lighted into a Room & I not being so good a Woodsman as ye rest of my Company striped myself very orderly & went in to ye Bed as they called it when to my Surprize I found it to be nothing but a Little Straw—Matted together without Sheets or anything else but only one thread Bear blanket with double its Weight of Vermin. I was glad to get up (as soon as y Light was carried from us) I put on my Cloths & Lays as my Companions. Had we not have been very tired I am sure we should not have slep'd much that night I made a Promise not to Sleep so from that time forward chusing rather to sleep in y open Air before a fire as will appear hereafter."

"Hoot, men," said the Scotchman. "That is an odd story. Pass the box, Joe, and don't forget Owler as the lord said."

The box went round from hand to hand. When it reached the Indian runner he merely said "Ugh," shook his head, and turned his face toward the roaring fire. The men laughed, old Nance bent over and shook her head, and the old lord continued his reading:

"*Fryday* 18th.—We Travell'd up about 35 Miles to Thomas Barwicks on Potomack where we found y. River so excessively high by Reason of y. Great Rains that had fallen up about y. Allegany Mountain as they told us which was then bringing down y. melted Snow & that it would not be fordable for severall Days it was then above Six foot Higher than usual & was rising we agreed to stay till Monday we this day call'd to see y. Fam'd Warm Springs we camped out in y. field this Night. Nothing Remarkable happen'd till sonday y. 20ᵗʰ."

"If he had had Harry Mendell's floating horse, there would have been no need of waiting," said Loveland, the overseer. "He could have gone right over on the water."

Nance shook her turban again.

"Hoot, man, that is no fair," said the Scotchman. "Harry is not here to speak for himself now."

Lord Fairfax continued:

"*Sonday* 20ᵗʰ finding y. River not much abated we in y. Evening Swam our horses over & carried them to Charles Polks in Maryland for Pasturage till y. next Morning."

"That is the way the boy got over," said one of the men.

"Hoot, man, one can't say now; there's mony strange happenin' in this queer world."

"*Monday* 21ˢᵗ.—We went over in a Canoe & Travell'd up Maryland side all y. Day in a Continued Rain to Collᵒ Cresaps right against y. Mouth of y. South Branch about 40 Miles from Polks I believe y. worst Road that ever was trod by Man or Beast."

"Hoot, men, hear that now," said the Scotchman.

"*Wednesday* 23ᵈ.—Rain'd till about two oClock &

Clear'd when we were agreeably surpris'd at y. sight
of thirty odd Indians coming from War with only
one Scalp. We had some Liquor with us of which
we gave them Part it elevating there Spirits put them
in y. Humour of Dauncing of whom we had a War
Daunce there manner of Dauncing is as follows Viz.
They clear a Large Circle & make a Great Fire in
y. middle then seats themselves around it y. Speaker
makes a grand Speech telling them in what Manner
they are to Daunce after he has finish'd y. best
Dauncer jumps up as one awaked out of a Sleep &
Runs & jumps about y. Ring in a most comicle Manner he is followed by y. Rest then begins there Musi-
cians to Play yᵉ Musick is a Pot half of Water with a
Deerskin Stretched over it as tight as it can & a
goard with some Shott in it to Rattle & a Piece of an
horses Tail tied to it to make it look fine y. one keeps
Rattling and y. other Drumming all y. while y. others
is Dauncing."

"Hoot, men! That is good. Joe, pass the box,
and don't forget Owler."

The young Indian again refused the snuff.

"*Fryday* 25ᵗʰ 1748.—Nothing Remarkable on thursday but only being with y. Indians all day so shall
slip it this day left Cresaps & went up to y. mouth
of Patersons Creek & there swam our Horses over got
over ourselves in a Canoe & travel'd up y. following

Part of y. Day to Abram Johnstones 15 Miles from yᵉ Mouth where we camped.

"*Saterday* 26ᵗʰ.—Travell'd up yᵉ Creek to Solomon Hedges Esqr one of his Majestys Justices of yᵉ Peace for yᵉ County of Frederick where we camped when we came to Supper there was neither a Cloth upon yᵉ Table nor a Knife to eat with but as good luck would have it we had Knives of own.

"*Saterday April* 2ᵈ.—Last Night was a blowing & Rainy night Our Straw catch'd a Fire yᵗ we were laying upon & was luckily Preserv'd by one of our Mens awaking we run of four Lots this Day which Reached below Stumps."

"Thunder weather," said old Nance.

"*Sunday* 3ᵈ.—Last Night was a much more blostering night than yᵉ former we had our Tent Carried Quite of with yᵉ Wind and was obliged to Lie yᵉ Latter part of yᵉ night without covering there came several Persons to see us this day one of our Men Shot a Wild Turkie."

"More thunder weather," said the negress mysteriously.

"*Monday* 4ᵗʰ this morning Mʳ Fairfax left us with Intent to go down to yᵉ Mouth of yᵉ Branch we did two Lots & was attended by a great Company of People Men Women & Children that attended us through yᵉ Woods as we went showing there Antick tricks I really think they seem to be as Ignorant a Set of People as the Indians they would never speak English but when spoken to they speak all Dutch this day our Tent was blown down by yᵉ Violentness of yᵉ Wind."

"All alone in the thunder weather," said old Nance. "How de wind moan, and moan, in de forest trees!" She bowed her head and shook her turban as in great distress, when a motion from the lord's hand brought her up straight as an arrow.

" *Thursday* 7ᵗʰ.—Rain'd Successively all Last night This Morning one of our men killed a Wild Turkie that weight 20 Pounds we went & Survey'd 15 Hundred Acres of Land & Return'd to Vanmetris's about 1 oClock about two I heard that Mʳ Fairfax was come up & at 1 Peter Casseys about 2 Miles of in yᵉ same Old Field. I then took my Horse & went up to see him we eat our Dinners & walked down to Vanmetris's we stayed about two Hours & Walked back again and slept in Casseys House which was yᵉ first Night I had slept in a House since I came to yᵉ Branch."

"Hoot, men, he worked weel," said the Scotchman. "Joe, pass the box on that. He did na shirk, he worked weel."

And again the snuff went round. One of the men sneezed, and the Indian started.

"What do that for?" asked the Indian.

7

"The powder *tickle*," said one of the men.

"*Powder!*" said Owler. "Blow his head off. Indian no take powder. Blow Indian's head up!"

"*Fryday* 8th.—We breakfasted at Casseys & Rode down to Vanmetris's to get all our Company together which when we had accomplished we Rode down below y[e] Trough in order to Lay of Lots there we laid of one this day The Trough is couple of Ledges of Mountain Impassable running side & side together for above 7 or 8 Miles & y[e] River down between them you must Ride Round y[e] back of y[e] Mountain for to get below them we Camped this Night in y[e] Woods near a Wild Meadow where was a Large Stack of Hay After we had Pitched our Tent & made a very Large Fire we pull'd out our Knapsack in order to Recruit ourselves every was his own Cook our Spits was Forked Sticks our Plates was a Large Chip as for Dishes we had none."

"Hoot, men, he did weel!" exclaimed the Scotchman. "Chips for plates. That wa' hard fare."

The Indian stared. He seemed afraid that the box of "powder" was to pass around again.

"*Tuesday* 12th.—We set of from Cap[t] Hites in order to go over W[ms] Gap about 20 Miles and after Riding about 20 Miles we had 20 to go for we had lost ourselves & got up as High as Ashbys Bent we did get over W[ms] Gap that Night and as low as W[m] Wests in

Fairfax County 18 Miles from ye Top of ye Ridge This day see a Rattled Snake ye first we had seen in all our journey.

"*Wednesday y^e* 13th *of April* 1748.—Mr Fairfax got safe home and I myself safe to my Brothers which concludes my Journal."

"That is good," said the Scotchman. "We'll all have a pinch of snuff on that."

Nance shook her turban.

Poor Owler understood the word *all.*

He held his nose, shook his head, and said:

"No loaded, no go off."

The men laughed. But in shaking the box rather violently one of the men caused the snuff to fly into the air. The Indian breathed it, lifted his head wildly, as though he thought he was about to explode, gave a tremendous sneeze, and leaped to his feet.

"Indian gone off," he said.

In a moment he was gone off indeed, and was never seen again in Greenway Court. What he reported to comrades in the wilderness can never be told.

"Hoot, men," said the Scotchman, "and that were strange. He thought it were powder now!"

"Washington is a brave boy," said the lord. "It is hardship that makes men. A man's power in life is in proportion to the resistance he meets when he is young. George will become a strong man one day."

The journal gives a correct view of the manner that the young surveyor passed a period of his early days. He was then scarcely more than a boy.

CHAPTER IX.

CHRISTMAS AT GREENWAY COURT—THE GOLDEN HORSESHOE.

CHRISTMASES on the old Virginia plantations before the Seven Year's War, as the Revolution was known, were scenes of festivity such as have seldom been seen elsewhere.

The aristocracy of the colony were, as a rule, rich and educated, and they loved English customs. The forests abounded in game and the meadows in cattle. Ships brought to the Chesapeake the luxuries of foreign ports. The yearly tobacco crops yielded large revenues. Most of the great plantations had many slaves, some of them a hundred or more each. These slaves as a rule were free on Christmas Day, and were allowed on every plantation to be with their superiors and masters during the merry-makings.

The literary entertainment on these days equalled the great dinner. Lord Fairfax had been a member of the *Spectator Club* in London, and had himself written articles for the *Spectator*. Shakespeare and

Milton were the favorite poets of the Virginia houses, and the musical frolic known as the "Beggars' Opera" furnished the merry songs on holiday occasions.

The fiddle was the favorite instrument. The Virginia gentry thought this instrument a fine accomplishment, and many of the young men played it well. The minuet was the courtly dance.

Story-telling was an art, and the natural story-tellers were the Dickenses and Thackerays of those primitive plantation days.

Christmas was a story-telling period. Smoking, fiddling, and merry tales led the Christmas mirth, and proud as the leading Virginians were, they shared their life in common with all people as well as their servants in the merry-makings of the Nativity.

It was Christmas night at Greenway Court. A story-telling party had been planned, which was to be followed by the burning of a great bonfire on a near hill. People gathered to the place from all the country round. Mr. Rouzé and Harry came; Mr. Gist was there, and the tall young form of George Washington.

The great fires roared in the chimneys and the tables were bright with light. Mr. Rouzé had promised to tell on this evening the story of "The Jolly Harper Man." The rooms became crowded and the fiddles set the air into rhythms. The slaves filled the great veranda and a few Indians were admitted inside.

Lord Fairfax looked happy. In his rude assembly he still maintained the grace of the court.

"There is something peculiar about that story that you are to tell to-night," he said to Mr. Rouzé.

"Yes, my Lord Fairfax, *very* peculiar."

"It is strange that I never heard the story. I have made a study of the ballads of the Border and like them. Here, take the arm-chair in the glow of the fire and begin. Let us have the secret of it, to which we have heard you refer until our curiosity is well whetted. My guests and friends and my boys of Greenway Court, all be seated. Mr. Rouzé is about to tell us a fine old story in the language of a ballad of the Scottish Border."

"Greenway Court!" The old lord gave such emphasis to the words that it brought to them all a sense of where they were. How beautiful the forest room looked to-night! The Baron of Cameron was a moral and religious man. He never forgot the old English Christmases, the waits and the madrigals. He had caused the Court to be hung with green. The walls were festooned with creeping pine and holly leaves and berries. From the rafters hung bunches of mistletoe and live-oak moss. The powder-horns and hunting-horns were arranged about the sideboard.

There were hemlock mattings behind the old English pictures. Greenway Court was a bower of green.

"The Boys of Greenway Court!" These were chiefly the young Virginia hunters and merry pioneers in whose society the old English lord and Baron of Cameron was always happy, and whom he treated with largest hospitality. But Washington, George William Fairfax, Mr. Gist, and the young fox-hunters, who chiefly belonged to the family of the gentry, were not all of the "boys." The Indian hunters loved the place and were welcome there. The young visitors from England who came out in ships to see the country sought the place, and were usually delighted with the timbered hills and sparkling waters of the Shenandoah. The sons of the provincial governors sometimes paid a visit to the place.

Lord Fairfax's wonderful pack of dogs had been brought from England. Under the Indian moons their voices rang out in the vast forests of those five million acres that the old lord was famed to possess. Their bay might be heard in the early mornings of all the frosty seasons when the cocks were crowing for day.

His hunting-horns made the hills echo. He loved the chase, and Washington sometimes accompanied him on his long hunting expeditions among the mountains.

After the episode of the runaway mare, Mr. Rouzé often became a guest of Greenway Court, and Harry, while yet under question, was made welcome there. Curiosity had caused him to be included at first, but later a half-belief that he was a victim of circumstances, and that his story might somehow be true, made the boy interesting to the lord. With the slaves Harry was not in favor. They called him Mr. Rouzé's " Riddle."

The Boys of Greenway Court were familiar with the old English hunting songs, and sang them to the blowing of horns and the baying of hounds. Tales of the English knights were here told to the music of the French harp and the sympathetic rhythms of fiddlers. Among these tales a favorite was the ballad of Chevy Chase, or the contest between Lord Percy and Douglas. This ballad had the air of the forest in it. Chaucer's tales were also favorites here and the Little Gist of Robin Hood.

Outside the Court pine-knots were smoking. The house was crowded and new visitors were arriving on horseback. Harry had found a place in one corner of the hall. The fiddlers now and then were playing snatches of lively airs, whose memory is still perpetuated in the Virginia reel.

Mr. Rouzé arose to recite the curious Scottish ballad. The fiddlers gathered around him to play be times during the pauses of the narrative. It was a pleasing feature of the old ballad story-telling for the fiddlers to play interludes and to adapt the music to the tone and spirit of the story. When the story-teller paused to make emphatic a sad episode, the fiddles took the minor tone, and when he paused amid a merry laugh at some humorous climax, the fiddles played merrily and brightened the gayety and the mirth.

As Mr. Rouzé was about to begin, the door was pushed slowly open and the head of an old woman appeared. The eyes of the merry-makers were turned toward her, and the old lord looked around.

"Is my boy here?"

The voice was thin, anxious, and pitiful.

Old Nance saw the woman and lifted her eyes and said with awe, "'Fore Gord!"

"That Mendell woman," said one. "What brings you here to-night?"

"She's cracked," said a thoughtless hunter.

"Hush," said the lord; "age and infirmity must be respected."

"May I come in?" asked the old woman pleadingly.

"Come to the fire, madam," said the lord, rising. "You have been travelling. I have here a party of young merry-makers keeping Christmas night, but it would ill become me not to give an aged woman a welcome on Christmas night.   Why do you come?"

"I know something.   The Lord has been revealing things to me.   I've got something."   She came out and stood by the fire.   She wore a shawl and a hood-like head-covering.   She pushed the hood back, and her white hair fell about her large, wrinkled fore-head.   She had some article concealed in a handker-chief.   She held it tightly.

"Sit down," said the lord, "and rest, and I will talk with you when you are warmed and rested."

He glanced at Harry, who was cowering in the cor-ner, knowing not what to do, and then said, "Now, Mr. Rouzé, we will listen to the story."

Mr. Rouzé raised his hand.   The old woman turned her head slowly, with a strange light in her gray eyes. "I've got it.   It's presents you give?   I've got a present for my boy.   The Lord has given it to me. This is a night of the Lord—gold, frankincense, and myrrh.   Is my boy here?   He ought to be.   His honor's as bright as any o' ye; as bright as yours, my Lord Fairfax.   This is a night of the Lord.   Mr. Rouzé, *look !* "

She began to unroll her handkerchief.

"Rest a little, madam," said the lord.   "We will hear you by and by.   Mr. Rouzé, we beg your par-don.   Now we are ready for the story."

There was a light strain from the fiddles, and Mr. Rouzé began:

THE JOLLY HARPER.

There was ane jolly harper man,
    That harpit aye frae toun to toun;
A wager he made, wi' two knichts he laid,
    To steal King Henrie's Bonnie Broun.

Sir Roger he wagered five ploughs o' lan',
    Sir Charles he wagered a thousand pound,
And John he's taen the deed i' han',
    To steal King Henrie's Bonnie Broun.

He's taen his harp into his han',
    And he gaed harpin' thro' the toun;
And as the king i' his palace sat,
    His ear was touchit wi' the soun'.

"Come in, come in, ye harper man,
    Some o' your harpin' let me hear."
"Indeed, my liege, an' by your grace,
    I'd rather hae stablin' for my meare."

"Ye'll gang to yon outer court,
    That stands a little below the toun;
Ye'll find a stable snug and neat,
    Where stands my statelie Bonnie Broun."

He's doun him to the outer court,
    That stood a little below the toun;

The jolly harper man.

There found a stable snug and neat,
   For statelie stood the Bonnie Broun.

Then he has fixt a guid strang cord
   Unto his gray mare's bridle rein;
And tied it unto that steed's tail,
   Syne shut the stable door behin'.

Then he harpit on, an' he harpit on,
   Till a' the lords were fast asleip;
Then doun thro' bouir and ha' he's gane,
   Even on his hands and feet.

         (Fiddles.)

He's to yon stable snug and neat,
   That lay a little below the toun;
For there he placed his ain gray meare,
   Alang wi' King Henrie's Bonnie Broun.

" Ye'll do you doun thro' mire an' moss,
   Thro' mony a bog an' miery hole;
But never miss youn Wanton slack,
   Ye'll gang to Mayblane to your foal."

As suin's the door he had unshut,
   The meare gaed prancin' frae the toun;
An' at her bridle rein was tied
   King Henrie's statelie Bonnie Broun.

Then she did rin thro' mire an' moss,
   Thro' mony a bog an' miery hole;
But never missed her Bonnie slack,
   Till she reached Mayblane to her foal.

When the king awakit frae sleip,
  He to the harper man did say,
" O! waken ye, waken ye, jolly John,
  We've fairly slept till it is day.

" Win up, win up, ye harper man,
  Some mair o' harpi' ye'll gie me."
He said, " My liege, wi' a' my heart,
  But first my gude gray meare maun see."

Then forth he ran, and in he cam',
  Droppin' mony a feignèd tear;
" Some rogues hae broke the outer court,
  An' stow'n awa' my gude gray meare."

" Then by my sooth," the king replied,
  " If ther's been rogues into the toun,
I fear as well as your gray meare,
  Awa's my statelie Bonnie Broun."

" My loss is great," the harper said,
  " My loss is twice as great, I feare;
In Scotland I lost a gude gray steed,
  An' here I've lost a gude gray meare."

" Come on, come on, ye harper man,
  Some o' your music lat me hear;
Weel paid ye'se be, John, for the same,
  An' likewise for your gude gray meare."

When that John his mony received,
  Then he went harpin' frae the toun;

But little did King Henrie ken
    He's stow'n awa' his Bonnie Broun.

The knichts then lay ower castle wa',
    An' they beheld baith dale an' doun;
An' saw the jolly harper man
    Come harpin' on to Striveling toun.
            (Fiddles.)
"Then by my sooth," Sir Roger said,
  "Are ye returnèd back to toun?
I doubt, my lad, ye hae ill sped
    O' stealin' o' the Bonnie Broun."

"I hae been into fair England,
    An' even into Lunnon toun;
An' in King Henrie's outer court,
    An' stow'n awa' the Bonnie Broun."

"Ye lee, ye lee," Sir Charles he said,
  "An' aye sae loud's I hear ye lee;
Twall armèd men in armour bricht,
    They guard the stable nicht and day."

"But I did harp them a' asleip,
    An' managed my business cunninglie;
If ye mak' licht o' what I say,
    Come to the stable an' ye'll see.

"My music pleased the king sae weel,
    Mair o' my harpin' he wished to hear,
An' for the same he paid me weel,
    An' also for my gude gray meare."

Then he drew out a gude lang purse
   Well stored wi' gowd an' white monie;
And in a short time after this
   The Bonnie Broun he lat them see.

Sir Roger produced his ploughs o' lan',
   Sir Charles produced his thousand pound;
Then back to Henrie, the English king,
   Restored the statelie Bonnie Broun.

During this recital the old woman had been un-
folding her handkerchief. As the ballad ended the
fiddlers began to play a merry air, and the old woman
started up.

"She's going to dance," said one of the young men,
laughing.

Nance shook her turban.

But she was not going to dance. The fiddles
ceased. All eyes were bent on the poor old woman.

"*That's* how it was, my Lord Fairfax. That's
how it was. The Lord revealed it to me last night
—Christmas Eve—and now he's revealed it to you
all. There are angels in the air on such nights as
these; angels in the air for those who can receive
them. 'He that hath ears to hear, let him hear.'
Lord Fairfax, did you ever doubt my boy's honor?"

"If I ever did, madam, it was when I was waiting
proof. I have a conviction that he is an honorable
lad. But, my good woman, what brings you here?"

"Lord Fairfax, listen! Reuben Rouzé, listen! George Washington, listen! You have all believed in my boy. I know you have. Heaven reward you all. Snuff the lights—snuff the lights! Reuben Rouzé, you have stood by the character of my friendless boy. Look *there!*"

She held up a horseshoe. It had a silver coating on one side, and on it was stamped the word "GAY."

The men gazed at it in silence. Harry started out of his hiding-place and came forward.

"Harry, O my own Harry! you are here. You are always in the heart of your poor mother. Do my eyes see you, Harry? You are here among these gentlemen."

"Among the boys of Greenway Court, my good woman," said the lord. "Now be calm. We are all your friends. No one shall harm you here. I would hold any woman to be noble who is seeking to protect her son's honor."

Lord Fairfax turned a half-reproving eye on his guests. He indicated that the old woman, as his guest, was to be treated with the respect due to her honest intentions.

She bent a fond look on Harry. "My boy," she said, "this is the last time. I shall never see ye again."

8

She stood there white and wrinkled, unkempt and uncared for, in the gleam of the great Virginia fire.

"Lord Fairfax, there is no room in the inn."

It was evident that her mind was wandering a little at times. She turned the horseshoe round and round. It glittered in the light as the silver marking came in view in the revolutions.

"Lord Fairfax, listen." She bent forward, holding her arm with the horseshoe aloft. "Lord Fairfax, where do you think I found it? Where do you think I found it? When I tell you that, you will know that every word that my boy said was true."

The room was silent. Every one bent forward with an eager look. She stood for a while in the same attitude, as silent as they. Old Nance stood with staring eyes.

"When I tell you where I found it," she said again, "you will know it all. I found it in the water. He said true. He was no dreamer. The horse did *not* swim. You will know all when I tell you. The *courier from Boston* was with me when I found it; he will tell you what I say is true."

For a moment she stood silent. "The courier from Boston, the courier from Boston," she repeated. She opened her mouth and stood speechless. The strain was too much. Her memory was going, her mind wandering. She put her hand on her fore-

Finding the evidence.

head and repeated, "The courier from Boston on his way to Williamsburg, the courier——"

"My good woman," said Lord Fairfax, "we are your friends. Collect your thoughts. Where did you get it?"

She stood like one dazed.

"I came to tell you, but it is all gone from me. My memory goes sometimes. It is gone. What was it I came to tell you? Who are you all? How did I come here? It is the last time—everything is so strange, and there is no room in the inn."

She dropped the horseshoe and sank down on the floor by the fire. Old Nance ran. A slave woman was called, and she led the old woman to one of the cabins. Harry followed her. The slave women made her comfortable.

It was indeed the last time. Paralysis, in a few hours, followed the mental failure.

"I wandered everywhere," she once said, "but I found it, I found it."

At midnight she said, starting up, "Mr. Rouzé! Bring him here. I must tell him *where* I found it."

Harry, who had not left her side, went for Mr. Rouzé. They stood around her. She was for a time unconscious. At last she opened her eyes like one returning to some strange place. She saw Harry.

"Oh, Harry, there is no room in the inn of this world for me. I have had a hard time, and I am going— Be true to the best that is in you, Harry—I was going to tell you where——"

She turned her head and lay perfectly still. The life storm was spent. She was *dead*.

CHAPTER X.

THE GOLDEN HORSESHOE.

THE exciting scene was followed by a long silence in the court. The old lord sat by the long oak table, his pipe in hand. Near him were George William Fairfax, George Washington, and Gist, the explorer. The gentry of the Northern Neck were there, and the sons of many Virginian families from Fredericksburg.

There was one young man there whom the old Baron of Cameron might proudly number among the boys of the Court. He was a son of Alexander Spotswood, or Spottswood, the beneficent governor of Virginia, whose administration closed in 1722.

The Virginians had hailed the inauguration of Governor Spottswood with great joy, and their faith in him was not disappointing. They sang:

> "He comes! his excellency comes
> To cheer Virginia's plains.

.   .   .   .   .   .

> Search every garden,
> Strip the shrubby bowers,
> And strew his path
> With sweet autumnal flowers.
>
> .   .   .   .
>
> And while Virginia is his care,
> May he protect the virtuous fair."

Governor Spottswood, unlike some former governors of Virginia, sought the public good. He was lib-
eral-minded, generous-hearted, and encouraged the
development of the country.

He organized a company of troopers to explore the
Blue Ridge, and led it in person to a point beyond
which no white foot had trod. On a high peak of
the Blue Ridge, from which he beheld the glorious
rivers and valleys that stretch toward the Ohio and
Mississippi, he inscribed his name, ALEXANDER
SPOTTSWOOD, and in commemoration of this event
George I. conferred upon him the honor of knighthood and presented him with a small gold horseshoe set with garnets and inscribed with the motto,
Sic jurat transcendere montes, "Thus he swears to
cross the mountains." The cavaliers of Spottswood
made the golden horseshoe their motto and wore it
in the palmy days of the great colonial governor.

Over the great fireplace of Greenway Court hung a

black velvet banneret, and on it was one of these golden horseshoes.

Black Joe, the body-servant of Lord Fairfax, stirred the wood coals as the silence became painful. The flames shot up, a spent log broke, and the coals rolled out on the hearth. The golden horseshoe on the velvet gleamed forth like a star.

"If the boy has indeed spoken the truth under such circumstances, when lies would have seemed to have served him so well," said Mr. Spottswood, "he ought to be knighted with a golden horseshoe."

"The golden horseshoe was bestowed on riders of honor," said George William Fairfax. "I would give one to a boy like that if his story proved to be true."

"You may give that to him some day if his story proves true," said the old lord. "It may come to you after I am gone. I love to look at it when it flashes forth the light of the lamp or when the coals fall out."

The men bent their eyes on the golden horseshoe.

"He will never get it," said Loveland, the overseer, breaking another silence: "horses in this age don't fly through the air or walk on the water. The days of miracles is gone, and if they were not that boy would not be called to perform them."

The guests departed. Midnight found Lord Fairfax sitting alone with the two Georges, and all somehow seemed to be thinking of the golden horseshoe.

The Christmas weather in Virginia is often bright and spring-like, like a farewell visit of summer days. It was so now, and old Lord Fairfax early sat down on the veranda the next morning in the cool and invigorating, but not uncomfortable, air. He was soon joined by Mr. Rouzé, who had spent the night at the Court.

"That was a strange thing that happened last night," said Lord Fairfax, "a very strange thing. And the old woman is dead and has not left any statement, they tell me, as to *where* she found the horseshoe. Have you examined the shoe?"

"Yes, and I feel sure that it is the one that was lost by the runaway horse. I can, I think, prove it to be so. There is only one blacksmith in Virginia that sets such shoes."

"Mr. Rouzé, your boy is friendless, but we owe it to our sense of honor and justice to investigate this case. There are things that every man owes to honor and justice. Will you take the poor woman's body back to Winchester, and see that she has a decent burial?"

Just then Washington came upon the veranda, and Lord Fairfax said to him: "Reuben Rouzé was born for the higher duties of life. Some men are. I have asked him to see that this strange affair of the Mendells be treated with charity and justice. Now,

George, Mr. Rouzé has shown himself in this matter
to be a wholly unselfish man. We must see that he
never wants for a friend."

"He shall never want for a friend if I can do him
any service."

"Such men as he," said the lord, "put all true men
under obligations to them. The world is their debtor.
May you never be a debtor to any one, Reuben
Rouzé! If you should, may you never want for a
friend!"

A number of young men had spent the night at
Greenway Court and its lodges to go on a hunting
party with Lord Fairfax. They gathered around the
old man and discussed the strange story of the horseshoe.

"I have no doubt," said Mr. Gist, "that the horseshoe belonged to Lawrence's horse and that it was
set by Collie, the blacksmith. But where the woman
found it will never be known. Nor can I see how
her story throws any light upon the truthfulness or
untruthfulness of the boy's story. The mare cast
a shoe: a deranged old woman found it: that is all."

"She did not find it floating upon the water, like
the prophet's axe," said the overseer sneeringly.

"But there is yet one person who may know where
she found it," said Mr. Rouzé.

"Who?" asked the overseer, who had not been

present when the old woman attempted to tell her story.

"The courier from Boston," said several voices.

"But," said the overseer, "no courier from *Boston* can ever make out that the horse ever crossed the Potomac on anything but a solid substance."

The statement appealed to the reason of all, and yet no one seemed satisfied.

"The woman," continued the overseer, "was simply out of her mind. You all seem to have faith in the boy. I tell you that he is a *rogue*. That is the whole story. That explains all things and makes all things clear. It is consistent with reason and nothing else is. This sympathy with a rogue is hardly consistent with the profession of——"

"*What*, sir?" asked Lord Fairfax.

The overseer had intended to say the word "gentlemen," but he saw that it was prudent to forbear.

He, however, added: "To sum up the whole thing: The old woman claimed to have found the horseshoe in some place that could prove her boy's story to be true. Now, in the first place the story itself is impossible, and, in the second place, she was crazy. The sympathy that I find expressed for the boy is wrong. The whole thing is simply ridiculous, and there does not live in these parts a more visionary man than Reuben Rouzé."

There was a silence among the young hunters. The overseer's remarks were impudent, but they had force.

The hunting party did not gather until the body of the poor woman had gone on its silent way to Winchester. Mr. Rouzé and Harry went with it. It had been placed in a long box with a blanket for a covering. Mr. Rouzé had taken the horseshoe with him to show to Mr. Lawrence. He still had faith in Harry against reason.

The funeral was a simple one, but after it a very strange event occurred.

There was an old colored man at the grave. He stared at Harry, and as soon as the rites were over he came up to him, shading his eyes mysteriously and saying:

"I's seen you befo', sure, I have now."

Harry's face lighted.

"Mr. Rouzé," said Harry, "I want you to listen to this man. It will help me."

"Do you want to know whar I's seen you befo'?"

"Yes," said Harry, "and I want this man to know. Speak."

"I's seen you by de light o' de lantern."

"Yes, but where? I am glad you are here."

"You was on a horse?"

"Yes."

" An oneasy critter, it was—heady?"

" Yes, yes!"

" I had been sent fo'."

" Yes."

" I tried to turn the animal. It wa'n't any use. I nebber did see an oneasy animal like ob dat!"

"Come with us," said Harry in an earnest tone. The three went to the home of Mr. Lawrence, near Winchester, among the Northern hills, and seated with Mr. Lawrence, the owner of the mare at the time of the Indian surprise, the old man told his simple tale.

After the story, which fully confirmed all that Harry had said, Mr. Lawrence examined the horseshoe and said to Mr. Rouzé:

"There is no doubt that Harry has told you the exact truth in every particular, as he understood it. The mare ran away. He could not prevent it. She thought that her colt was at Greenway Court and was determined to go there. This shoe belonged to the mare. You need not go to the blacksmith to identify it. I know it as well as he. How the mare crossed the river I do not know; but she did so, where there was no bridge. The boy thinks that she crossed in the way he told you. He is an honest lad. His father must be taken into our care. He cannot live long. I would hire Harry to work for me, but it will be for the boy's interest to remain with you.

"If we only knew where Harry's mother found the horseshoe," continued Mr. Lawrence, "the case might be perfectly clear."

"Yes," said Mr. Rouzé, "she spoke in such a confident tone that I have never doubted that she had a key to the whole mystery. But I am able to prove now that Harry did not steal the mare, and that he could not help the course that she took. There only remains one point in his statement that is not perfectly clear: it is that the horse seemed to walk on the surface of the water, and that he could see the water under him in the light of the moon as it broke through the clouds. There is only one person who can make this clear, and that is the *courier from Boston*. Who was he? He probably carried dispatches from the Governor of Massachusetts to the Governor of Virginia."

"But, Mr. Rouzé," said Mr. Lawrence, "don't you see that the boy seems to stand against his own interests in continuing to tell his story in this way? If he were dishonest or untruthful, he would give up the story or change it. He knows this! I tell you the boy is honest through and through. He comes of honest stock.

"Harry, look here. Search yourself through and through. Find out what is best in you and live for that. Time is the friend of truth."

Mr. Rouzé, on his return, communicated to Lord Fairfax these incidents.

"The boy is honest," said the old lord, pounding his cane, "and I shall invite him here among the boys of Greenway Court. I have been misjudged myself. Washington himself is not more honorable than this friendless boy. I shall stand by him. But I would give many a crown to hear the *courier from Boston* tell his story. Here is a riddle indeed. I may know some day; if not, you may."

Harry's invalid father became the charge of Mr. Lawrence, and Harry himself found a father in Mr. Rouzé.

CHAPTER XI.

WHEN a body comes to see Massa Fairfax," old Nance used to say, "den dar arises up a great bow-wow among the hills o' the Shenando'."

Old Nance spoke truly. Lord Fairfax, as we have intimated, owned the finest dogs that probably were to be found in the colonies. A part of these dogs were fox-hounds, a part companion dogs. One of the latter, a greyhound, was named Fernandino, and was called " Nan." This dog was the companion of old Nance, and had become a favorite among the people for an odd habit which he had learned from his mistress, of which we will speak.

Lord Fairfax loved to relate wonderful stories. Sitting with his pipe under the long, cool eaves of the veranda, it gave him pleasure to recall the legends of his ancestors, who had lived in his quaint house or Court of Nun-Appleton and in Leeds Castle. To picture old scenes and incidents took him in fancy back to England again. The long afternoons in the

Shenandoah often found him engaged in entertaining a visitor who had come from forty or more miles on horseback to see him. Men made long journeys to visit in those days, sometimes journeys of hundreds of miles, and they stayed long when they came; not a day or two, but a week or month. The Virginian houses had great barns and stables then, and hospitality was held to be privilege.

Old Nance delighted to listen to these castle tales. She was a favored slave at the Court, as she had the charge of the setting of the tables. She was very black and her turban was always very white, and she thought herself possessed of special spiritual sight or to be a kind of prophetess.

When the old lord began to tell quaint English wonder-tales on the veranda, she would come out of her cabin cautiously, making signs to the other negroes to be still. She would steal up to one corner of the Court within hearing, bow her white-turbaned head, and listen. Nan, the dog, would follow her, and he would hearken too.

Old Nance for a time used to listen to these tales out of sight of the lord. But Nan was a very sympathetic dog, and when a fearful legend approached a crisis and the old lord's voice took on an awesome tone, he would howl. This betrayed them both, and sometimes brought a reprimand from Loveland, the overseer. It was a ious sight, old Nance and Nan crouched down to er around the corner of the Court, the former ing a story and the latter apparently as full of s athy as his mistress herself.

Whenever Lord fax told a ghost-story Nance appeared to be gre moved and bobbed her head up and down and s ok it in the agony of nervous terror and excitem Nan would throw back his head to howl, but N ce would turn it back again by a sudden sweep of l black hand. The little negro boys would watch t e two with open mouths, and never were they so happy as when the old lord's voice became slow and solemn and he began to speak of some tragic deed of Lord This or Lady That.

"Wot will Nance and Nan do now?" they would say to each other.

If Nance saw this interest on the part of the "little coons," as she called the children, she would rise up, wave her arms mysteriously, and whisper, "Be still now. Sh-u-u, sh-u-u—or the thunder weather will get ye. Sh-u-u."

The tempests in the Shenandoah were sometimes fearful. The thunder would echo among the mountains and the rain fall in sheets. So the words "thunder weather" were particularly quieting to the negro children.

9

When Nan had first seen Harry Mendell crying, he set up a howl that echoed among the hills. Old Nance said that it was a sign.

"The dog knew," said she. "He knew for shor" (sure).

"Who yo' suppose tol' him?" asked old Joe, the lord's faithful body-servant.

"Tol' 'im? I'll tell ye, ole Nance knows. She is gifted wid de secrets of natur'. Who tol' 'im? The horse tol' 'im. Animals talk to each other. Tell things. You can't hear 'em. _I_ can. Ole Nance has hearin' ears. _Come from the Lord._"

Nan continued to howl whenever Harry first appeared.

"Did ye hear dat?" old Nance would say. "Wot I tell ye? Nan knows it all. He could tell if he could only speak. I overheard the bay horse a-talkin' to him—the horse wot the boy stole; there now, for shor."

The negroes believed the accusation. They shrank away from Harry whenever he came to the place. He felt the unfriendliness keenly.

There was an alarm-bell on the top of the Court. It was rung in danger and to call the riders together on fox-hunting days. Harry was from time to time sent to the Court by Mr. Rouzé in the interest of the planters on the neck between the two rivers, and whenever black Nance saw him coming she would ring the bell.

Once on being reproved for doing so she said:

" He is a thief.   Wot dat bell fo', I'd like to know? Didn't the lord tell us all to ring it when danger come?   Wot dat bell fo'?"

One day in early summer Lord Fairfax was sitting on the veranda.   The locust trees were in bloom and their odors filled the air.   The swallows or swifts were darting about the sunny meadows and the Baltimore orioles were fluting around their pouched nests in the high trees.   Afar rose the mountains, purple at morning and evening, but now shimmering in golden light in the sun.

The old lord was entertaining some hunters on the veranda, and Nance and Nan were listening in the cool shadow of the gambrel roof that fell across the way.

"My ancestress, the Lady Isabel," said Lord Fairfax, "was captured from a nunnery in the times of Henry VIII.   The abbess had resolved to make a nun of her in order to retain her fortune, but Sir William came down on the convent with a troop of horse and carried her away to Bolton Percy Church, and there they were married."

So much of the story had been not very clear to Nance, and Nan had comprehended about as much of it as his turbaned mistress.

"But," continued the lord, lowering his voice, "Sir William made a very mysterious will."

Nance shook her turban, and Nan threw back his head to howl over the dark scenes of the Courtly Ages, when his mistress gave him a cuff on the ear, saying, "Sh-u-u."

"A *very* mysterious will."

Nance and the dog were all attention now. The emphatic word *very* made them all ears.

"It read like this: note it well——"

Nance put her hand to her ear. The hound pricked up his ears in imitation, and the negro children stood open-mouthed in the doors of the shady cabins.

"'First,' he wrote, 'I bequeath my soul to the Lord Jesus.'"

Nance shook her turban and Nan was about to howl, when he received another cuff and took a respectful attitude again.

"'—and my body to be buried in Bolton Church.'"

Where Bolton Church was Nance had not the faintest idea and Nan knew no better, but the words were so poetic that Nance shook her turban and Nan was about to howl, when the latter received the usual correction.

"'—And let my executors see,'" continued the lord, quoting the will, "'that my dead body is brought forth

Old Nance.

from the church by fourteen poor men, wearing black gowns and carrying torches.'"

This Nance could partly understand.

She shook her head in her usual way, bending over, and shut down the dog's head as the latter lifted his nose into the air. The children began to make an outcry at the door of one of the cabins.

"Be still dar," she said in a low voice. "Be still, I tells ye. Be still and saw wood, now sh-u-u."

Just what poor Nance meant by the direction, "and saw wood," no one ever knew. It was one of her refrain words, by which she sought to make all orders to silence emphatic.

"But the strange part of the story is yet to come," said the old lord. "Sir William ordered further that thirteen shillings should be paid to these fourteen frocked mourners, and that every man but one should have a shilling."

"And who was he who should *not* have a shilling?" asked a visitor.

"Guess, my good friend."

"I cannot tell," said the guest.

"It was to be he who should mourn the *least*. So," added the old lord, "the fourteen men began to mourn, and a doleful time they made of it. They made the highway wail. The first said 'Ah-a—me.'"

Old Nance bent her head toward the ground at that

word of deep mystery and awe, and she gave her turban such a shake to indicate that she understood the
occult meaning of the word that the distressed dog
got his head well set back and his mouth well open
and uttered an ear-piercing howl.

The dogs in the kennels began to bark, and amid
this unexpected awakening of life the figure of a
young man on horseback appeared on the way leading
down to the Court.

"Dat Mendell boy," said old Nance. She was
about to pull the bell-rope, but saw that the lord was
continuing his story.

She spoke to Nan.

"*Howl*," said she.

The poor dog obeyed. The dogs in the kennels
answered the dismal cry, and amid the confusion
caused by these sounds Harry rode into the yard.

The little colored children ran into their cabins.
The dogs that were loose eyed the young rider suspiciously.

"You are welcome," said Lord Fairfax. "You
have come to learn about the arrangements for the
fox-hunt?"

"Yes," said Harry. "Mr. Rouzé sent me for the
planters."

The welcome of the old lord was most cordial, but
the general atmosphere of the place made Harry un-

happy as usual.   The black groom took his horse to
the stable with a look of distrust.   The heads of the
negroes were seen at the doors of the cabins, looking
out sidewise.   When old Nance passed him on the
veranda to lay the covers on the table, she said with
a leer, "Stranger things has happened.   We'll hab
thunder weather now for shor!"

Harry saw that Nance and Joe, who worked in the
house at meals, were reluctant to serve him at the
table.   He fancied that even the other guests had
heard his story and treated him with reserve.

After supper the guests departed on horseback for
a long ride by moonlight through the Virginia forests.
Harry was left alone with Lord Fairfax.   Harry was
depressed by the incidents that had occurred.

"Why are you so lonely, my boy?" said the lord.

"My Lord Fairfax, I live under suspicion all the
time, and I am not to blame.   I can bear to be poor,
to work hard, and to suffer anything that misfortune
can bring that leaves me honor.   But to be suspected
of being a thief and a liar is more than I can endure.
I think of it all the time."

He was silent and the old lord whiffed his pipe.

"Pardon me, my Lord Fairfax, you have been
very kind to me.   You are good and just to everybody.
Pardon me—but did you ever have any trouble?"

"You are bold, my boy, but you mean well.   What

you really are craving for is sympathy. I understand it all. My heart is as human as yours, and I have suffered——"

The old lord became silent. He held his pipe in his hand.

"My boy, I have suffered. I can feel for you. The heart of a baron and the heart of an orphan are the same.

"My boy, I have a parchment which I have hidden in the garret from the eyes of the world. It will be found some day after I am gone.* It is a marriage contract. I have effaced the lady's name, for she cast me off after the wedding-day had been appointed.

"My boy, why do I tell you this? Why? The gay world used to look at me askance. I remember how I used to feel. It was that that drove me to the wilderness. That is why I am here. I carry a shadow with me. Every man casts a shadow. The man has a dead heart who does not cast a shadow. Boy, I pity you. But, my boy, my boy, I do believe in your honor. You are honest at heart."

Harry's eyes filled with tears.

"Pardon me—if I have a right to expect such treatment from you. Why do you believe in my honor, my Lord Fairfax? My own word is against me."

*It was so found by some children at play.

"You carry with you the tone and atmosphere of sincerity, my boy. An honest man can discern such things. He has eyes to see what is honest. And I am not an exile for any dishonor. I am an honest man."

"You have faith, my lord?"

"Yes, faith."

"Faith that there is a Power that will do justice to all in the end?"

"Yes, I have that faith. My boy, I know not why I have been led into the wilderness; but I have faith that it is for some good purpose. It may be that my influence on my cousin, or on Washington, or on you may lead to good results. My boy, I cannot see the way, but I can trust my guide. I have not been sent here by Providence for nothing. Why it is I cannot tell, but I have the purpose that the Virginia families in this wilderness shall be better for me."

The boy looked in awe on the great, dark-faced man as he sat before him. He had seen how his thoughts had influenced Washington and the young men who came to visit him.

"My boy, do you need money? I am a generous man, they say. I mean to be."

"No, my lord, I do not desire money until my character stands clear in the eyes of the world."

"You would not mind my giving you a few guineas?"

"Yes, my lord. No money can make me happy as I am now. To take money now would make me seem to be willing to be dependent in the eyes of the world."

"You are right, my boy. A person on the defensive should not be made dependent by receiving any favor. You are right.

"Harry Mendell, your character will make your case clear some day. No one can injure one's character but one's self, and the time has compensations for everything that the innocent suffers.

"My boy, the height is in proportion to the depth, and character is everything. I wish that your story could be proven true; your character then under the circumstances would be the highest that I have ever found in all the Virginia wilderness, and we are growing *men* here; I know not for what purpose, but we are growing men here."

The two sat together. Old Nance came in darkly and tidied up the room. A calumet hung by the fireplace in which the fire was dead, and over it was the golden horseshoe on a velvet banneret. A dim light fell on these objects, but the rest of the room was in shadow.

Old Nance went out silently, and a bat flew in and dashed about the room.

"My boy," said the lord, "I am a lonely old man, a lonely old man. I am glad that you have come. I love to feel a friendliness for you. I am a lonely old man; I know not why; it is for some good purpose—perhaps the lives of the young men who come here may yet reveal the cause. God only knows."

The moon hung over the mountains. There was quiet in the cabins, and the great valley was bright and still. Harry went to rest that night with an irresistible purpose to prove his story true. The conviction that he owed it to himself to do this grew upon him.

CHAPTER XII.

BLACK NANCE'S MIRACLE.

BLACK NANCE had heard the Scriptures read at the Court and the Episcopal clergyman preach at Winchester. The poetic part of any religious service appealed to her, and she thought that she saw visions and received messages from the skies. Her sharp eyes, ebony face, and high turban gave her the appearance of a leader, and when she declared to the slaves in the cabins that she was a "called woman," a "selected branch from the topmost tree," the sable colony began to regard her with awe and to consult her on all questions in which they lacked wisdom.

She claimed to be a prophetess and the colored people believed in her prophecies. She enjoyed her power over them, and if any one doubted her or disobeyed her, she quickly brought such an one to a sense of dependence by saying, "Take care, you better look out now; ole Nance can *cast an evil eye.*" She would then fix her black eye on the rebel against her authority and bring him to terms.

She gathered up a few figures of the Scripture, enlarged them and put her own meanings upon them, and began to teach and to preach.

It was her delight to go on Sunday afternoons to some majestic trees on the Shenandoah, a few miles away, and there meet the colored people of the valley and to relate her visions and to prophesy. The trees were the patriarchs of the primeval forest. The river wound under their great mossy branches like a ribbon of silver, and the fields of prairie grass around them waved brightly in the summer wind. This grass grew to be five feet high, and a rider on horseback could in some places tie the heads over his horse's back. It was sprinkled with flowers and was full of the songs of birds in the early summer-time.

One day old Nance gathered around her the people of the cabins and said:

"Nex' Sunday, in de middle of the art'noon, I will prophesy under the trees. I have had a wision."

The announcement caused immediate interest.

"I have had a wision; it was about dat dar Mendell boy whose horse walked on de water."

The interest grew. She saw that she had awakened curiosity and was filled with delight and pride at a sense of her power.

She lifted her long, dark arm, spread open her fingers, bent forward her head with its tall white turban, and said:

"Ole Nance could walk upon de waters of the Shenando' if de people only have faith.   Come and see!"

She stood silent.   The negroes were mute.   They stood motionless with staring eyes.

She turned around and marched back to her cabin with a slow, measured step.   The mute figures watched her.   At last one of the negroes ventured to say, "Ole Nance is gwine to walk on de water of de Shenando' nex' Sunday.   I'll be dar."

"And I," "and I," said one after another.   The news flew.   The appointment was soon known in all the negro cabins around Greenway Court.

Old Nance had seen the wonder that Harry Mendell's story had awakened and she was jealous of it. She had resolved to prophesy against the boy.

There was a large gathering of the colored people under the big trees of the Shenandoah to hear old Nance prophesy and to see her walk on the water.

She came to the place alone, her high white turban on her head and a look of confidence in her bony face. It was a lovely day in June.   A light wind blew over the tall grasses, revealing the colors of flowers.   The river lay clear under the banks of prairie grass and the shadows of the giant trees.

The negroes received old Nance in silence.   Their

minds were filled with a superstitious awe. They seemed to be all eyes before she put her hand up to her forehead and began to prophesy, and all ears as soon as she had opened by crying "Childern ob de wilderness, where am you, childern ob de wilderness?"

She pretended not to see them.

"Here, here," exclaimed many voices.

"Childern ob de wilderness, where am you?" She stretched out her right arm and seemed to be feeling for them in air.

"Here, 'ere," shouted the company in a louder voice.

"Wot is dat I hear? Am dat yo', childern ob de wilderness?"

"Here, 'ere," cried the excited company in a louder voice.

"Childern ob de wilderness, listen!"

She had no need of these awesome words. The negroes stood around her like so many ebony statues.

"I hab had a wision in de watches ob de night. O ye childern ob de wilderness, let me hab yo' ears."

The young negroes may have wondered if this last request was to be taken literally, and they were relieved when, after an impressive silence, they found it but a figure of speech. "I hab had a wision in de watches ob de night. A voice came to me when de new moon was mowin' de fields ob de heabens. An' wot yo' think it said? You no can tell? No, yo' no can tell. It said, O childern ob the wilderness; listen now—it said that dat Mendell boy was a false speaker; dat he no walk his horse on de water; it said, 'Go out under de big trees ob de Shenando' and prophesy against him;' an' de new moon was a-mowin' de harbest fields of de heabens."

She then in a series of awful figures proceeded to picture the sad end of those who have false tongues and false hearts. She predicted that the world would speedily be destroyed by a tempest and exhorted them to prepare for the day when the last tempest should come.

In the midst of her frantic exhortation a black cloud loomed over the hills and there was heard a distant rumble of thunder. The appearance seemed to awe her and to make her question herself, if she after all were quite sincere.

The cloud passed, leaving a few broken fragments in the sky. She ended her prophecy with a command which had come to her "from de skies," while the "new moon was mowin' de heabens," that "de childern ob de wilderness" should all shun "dat boy Harry Mendell" and themselves follow the "spirit of the trut'" (truth).

"And now," she said, "ole Nance am gwine to walk upon de waters ob de Shenando'."

Some of the negroes shrieked at this declaration. Others fell on their knees or stood with lifted hands. The very dogs caught the spirit of the moment of excitement and hid themselves as from a spectre behind their masters. Nance turned her face toward the river. An hysterical woman, sinking down on the ground, exclaimed "Fo' the land's sake!" and uttered a piercing shriek.

"Wot you shriek fo'?" said old Nance. "I said I could walk upon de waters ob de Shenando' if de people hab faith to believe. Don't yo' believe? I can't walk if yo' don't believe.

"Childern ob de wilderness, I can't walk if yo' don't believe. Didn't I tell ye so? How many ob ye believe dat ole Nance can walk on de waters ob de Shenando'? Cry up loud now, ye childern ob de wilderness. How many ob ye believe?"

There arose a great shout. Every voice exclaimed "I!"

"Den if you all believe it, wot is de need of my walkin' at all on de waters ob de Shenando'? We will all go home believin' and rejoicin' in de knowledge of de trut'."

The company returned silently and thoughtfully, but with a prejudice against "dat Mendell boy."

"I knew dat de powers would lead me through," said old Nance as she sat in the door of her cabin that

10

night. "This has been a hard day for me, but I hab been delivered out ob all ob my troubles."

And she whiffed her pipe. She was not wholly insincere. She half believed in herself. Her desire to be regarded as a wonder-worker had persuaded her that she was one, and that her inconsistencies were somehow a part of an inspirational life. She was happy in believing herself to be the prophet of the Shenandoah.

CHAPTER XIII.

THE WOLF-HUNT.

CALL out all the hunters. Tell them to meet me at the White Post on Saturday. I will give fifty guineas to the man who will capture or kill that wolf!"

The speaker was Lord Fairfax. He gave the order to Loveland. News had come to Greenway Court that morning that a timber-wolf had made shocking havoc among a flock of sheep in the hill pastures. The wolf had only eaten a part of one sheep, but he had killed many. The same timber-wolf, it was supposed, had made like depredations before. He had been seen twice in the hill fields. Wolves usually go in packs, but in this case a solitary animal was believed to be the cause of the slaughter of the flocks on the hill pastures of Greenway Farm.

This "White Post" named by Lord Fairfax stood in an open way a mile or two from the Court. It was a guide-post that pointed the way to Greenway Farm. A white post stands on the same place to-day. We recently saw it. A village called White Post grew up

around it, and the people have always been proud of
the traditions of this curious octagon except those
which claim it was once used as a whipping-post.
A ride of a few miles out of Winchester will bring one
to the White Post.

Lord Fairfax called a postman.

"Go to Mr. Rouzé," he said. "Ask him if he will
allow Harry Mendell to tell the hunters around Fredericksburg that there will be a wolf-hunt on Saturday,
starting from the White Post, and that I will pay
fifty guineas for the head of a certain timber-wolf."

The postman was a colored man. Old Nance heard
the order.

"There be hunters enough here, Massa Fairfax."

"What do you mean? Why do you say that to me?
Go."

"Massa Fairfax, I've been warned."

"What do you mean?"

"I've been warned against dat boy Harry Mendell."

Old Nance appeared before the lord, her high turban bobbing.

"Massa Fairfax, I has prophesied against him. I
did, now, on de day dat I walked on de waters ob de
Shenando'."

"Not a word more of this foolish superstition. Go!"

The postman was soon seen flying over the hills
and Nance went about her domestic concerns with a

sullen humiliation. "Drat dat boy!" she said. "De white folks all believe in him. But his day am comin'. I'll make it come. Ole Nance can see. She knows."

Saturday came. It was a late April day and the boughs of the trees wore the colors of early spring. Some of the young hunters from Fredericksburg had arrived at the Court the evening before and had been bountifully feasted.

Mr. Rouzé and Harry came to the Court late at night. When Harry appeared in the court-yard in the morning, the negroes fled into the cabins in terror and only ventured to look at him through the shutters or cracks in the logs. Old Nance had made a deep impression on their minds on the day that she, as she said, "walked on de waters of de Shenando'."

The yard of the Court was filled with lusty young riders and splendid horses early in the morning. An hour or so later all of the hunters had assembled at the White Post.

There was a blowing of horns, a prancing of proud, restless horses, and a baying of hounds. The roads were muddy, but the hillsides were rocky and firm, and the riders, led by Lord Fairfax, soon mounted the hills. The dogs had scented the timber-wolf before and followed the scent to some high rocks among the hills. They seemed to understand the purpose of the hunt to-day. They led the horses and took the course that led to the same high rocks in the timber.

The hounds stepped on the long ridge of the rocks, bayed, and pawed the earth with their feet. The hunters gathered around them.

Near the place was found some wool from one of the sheep in the hill pastures. But there was no other trace of the prey.

The hunters began to move forward, but the hounds did not respond to the call.

"The wolf is here," said the old lord. "There is some cave here; the earth is hollow under us. The tone of the hounds is proof of this."

But where was the entrance to the cave?

"If the wolf have a den here," said Mr. Rouzé, "the hole that leads down to it must be easy to find. And," he added, "I have found it! Here it is under the shelf of this rock."

"Is it large enough to enter?" inquired the lord.

"No, the dogs could not enter it. See here."

He tore away some bushes. The dogs rushed to the place, and one after another forced his head into the hole and drew back barking in a fever of excitement. Mr. Rouzé tore away the earth and let the light into the crevice.

"Here is a small hole leading down into the earth," he said. "Only a small dog could enter it. A grey-

hound might force his way down there; one with a
very thin body like Nan."

"'There is a wolf's den in these rocks," said the
lord, "and here is the source of the mischief to the
flocks. Can the rocks be broken and lifted?"

The hunters tried to break and lift the rocks on the
surface. They did so to a little depth, revealing a
hole in the solid rock like the flue of a chimney.
There was a hollow cave beneath, as was indicated
by the conduct of the hounds and the echo there of
the sounds from above.

"No one can ever kill that wolf in his den," said
Mr. Rouzé. "No dog here can crawl down into that
hole to drive him out."

"Let me send for Nan," said Lord Fairfax. "Harry,
go back for Nan and we will lunch here."

Harry rode down the hills, and the hunters were
provided with refreshments.

Before the party lay the wonderful valley, walled
with mountains and sparkling with the winding waters
of the Shenandoah. Here were forests of giant trees;
there prairies of old yellow grass, amid which the new
green grass was springing. A line of blue lay along
the high hills and the far mountains seemed like peaks
of the sun.

"I have no wish ever to go again beyond the mountains," said Lord Fairfax, looking down on the en-

chanting scene. "The world lies beyond the mountains, and I have no wish ever to mingle with the
world again. My world is here. Nature is my companion and book of study, and nature to me is more
than any art."

When Harry Mendell was seen flying on horseback
down to Greenway Court, the negroes ran into the old
lord's stone study and fastened the door, and old
Nance rang the bell on the roof.

Harry found Nan in the yard. Nance had fled to
her cabin and left the terrified dog outside. He called
the dog after him, and as Nance did not dare to give
a counter-order from the cracked logs of her cabin,
Nan obeyed. The boy, horse, and dog were soon flying up the hills, and the negroes came out of their
hiding-places and gathered around the Court with in-
terrogation-points in their eyes.

Nance came out of her cabin and the negroes waited
her word.

"Wot I tell yo'? He *lit* right down here and carried off the dog like a hawk out ob de open sky. Wot
I tell yo'? He's conjured, but I can sot a spell upon
him. Yo' trust me. Old Nance will sot a spell upon
him. Nan!"

She threw up her arms.

"Nan! Where's yo' gone? Nan, my dog Nan, ole
Nance will nebber see yo' any more! Nan! Nan!"

The negroes knew not what to make of these things. Nance went into her cabin and shut the door, saying, " These be the days ob signs and wonders! dese be the las' times!''

When Nan arrived at the cave he entered at once into the excitement. He was a tall dog, but his body was hardly bigger around than a spaniel's. He belonged to a rare and peculiar breed of greyhounds, and his graceful form had won the old lord's eye and his sympathetic howl made him a favorite on the farm. For this reason he had given him over to the care of old Nance, who looked after the spreading of his tables. The old lord had several curious dogs, and these he put in the special charge of trusty slaves.

Nan put his head into the rocky hole and drew back and howled. The tone of his voice showed that there was game below.

The dogs followed Nan's example, and again one after another tried to enter the hole, but each drew back baffled.

Nan was now quivering with excitement. He put his head down into the hole again, and his body began to disappear like the going down of a serpent into a hole in the earth. In a few minutes he was out of sight.

What would happen next? The men waited to see him return. They ordered the dogs to be still.

At last the dogs seemed to scent some new cause of excitement and could hardly be restrained from crowding upon the crevice again. There was something living in the top of the hole. A head, ears, eyes.

The head drew back. The animal saw the enemy before it, but an enemy was behind it. It was the timber-wolf.

The head came out again.

"Fire," said the old lord.

A dozen guns puffed. The wolf was dragged out of the hole dead. The hunt had been short, exciting, and successful. But where was Nan?

A piteous howl was heard in the hollow below, but the dog did not appear.

Harry called to him: "Nan! Nan!"

The howl was repeated.

"The dog is in pain," he said.

Mr. Rouzé called at the mouth of the crevice. Nan answered.

"The dog is disabled," he said. "Listen!"

"Nan!"

The same piteous howl answered back.

One after another the hunters called down. The same cry answered them all.

"What are we to do?" asked Mr. Rouzé.

"We cannot enter the cave," said Lord Fairfax. "We must leave the dog there for the present. He

will work his way out and come home. I will have
Joe visit the place if he does not come home. Nan
shall not suffer."

When the hunters returned to the Court and old
Nance and the negroes heard of the fate of Nan, there
was lamentation and mourning indeed. Nance went
about, bent double, uttering a dismal sound without
words.

Harry remained at the Court after the home hunters had gone and made arrangements to spend the
night there. But his thoughts were fixed upon
Nan.

Whatever may have been the superstitions of old
Nance, she had a tender heart for her dog. She
looked out of her cabin door and saw Harry passing.

"Yo' go 'long. Yo' carry off my dog. Nebber a
wink will I sleep to-night. I can hear Nan cryin' and
cryin' and cryin' down in yarth there among de animals. I can hear and ebbry cry drives a nail into my
heart. Yo' go 'long. If yo' wa'n't conjured, I make
yo' take me to de cabe where Nan is moanin', moanin'. Who yo' think Nan is thinkin' about now? Nan
is thinkin' ob me. Many's de happy hour I's spent
wid dat dog. Now he's buried alive in de hollows
of de yarth. I sot just as much store by dat dog as
by one ob my own childern. Yo' go 'long."

Harry went to his room and bed. But he could not

sleep. The sound of Nan's voice rang in his ears and haunted him, and old Nance's words worried and distressed him.

He got up in the night and went back to the hills. It was full moon now and the valley was almost as bright as day.

He went to the place where Nan had been left. He called again at the top of the passage that led to the cavern. There was no answer.

"Nan! Nan!"

No answer.

He drew back and rested.

What was that?

There came a low, pitiful cry from some bushes below. It was repeated.

He climbed down the rocks and listened. He heard a patter of feet. It was followed by a howl of distress.

"Nan!"

An animal broke the bushes and fell down before him panting. It was Nan. He had made his way out of an unknown entrance to the cave. His front legs were torn and bleeding, and one of them was broken.

Harry took the faithful dog up in his arms and carried him back to the Court. Nan had had an encounter with a wolf in the cave. But if the wolf that

had been killed had disabled him, why did that animal seek to escape?

Harry went back to the place in the morning and
found the new entrance, and that doubtless another
wolf had been in the cave and attacked Nan after the
dog had driven the first wolf out through the hole.
The sound of the guns may have led the other wolf to
escape. Nance took Nan into her cabin, and no child
could have been more tenderly nursed.

Who should receive the fifty guineas? Lord Fairfax was one of the judges in the courts of the Shenandoah and was regarded as very just and wise, but
here was a difficult case for decision.

He gave a dinner the next day to the hunters.
People who came far to make visits in the old Virginia
days stayed long and were abundantly feasted. This
was the Golden Age of Virginia, as the eighteenth
century there was afterward called; the "days of Ar-
cady." Hospitality made men happy then, and to
give bountifully was the characteristic of the gentry
of the old school; tables groaned.

After the feast came the fiddles, and after the fiddles
the pipes on the veranda, and after the pipes the conference in regard to the award.

The hunters decided in answer to the lord's questions that the twelve men who fired upon the timber-
wolf ought to share the award between them.

The twelve men considered the matter. It was Nan that had driven the wolf out of the hole. They decided to give the award to the kennel-keeper to be spent for the comfort of Nan.

"I will care for Nan," said the old lord.

"Then let the award be given to Harry Mendell," said one of the hunters. "The dog merits the reward, and he was the best friend of the dog."

To this all agreed, and Harry Mendell was called into the impromptu court and received the fifty guineas.

Men rode long distances in the evenings in those days and stopped late at night at wayside inns. At the dusk of the long day, Mr. Rouzé and Harry prepared to start for the first inn on the way to Fredericksburg.

Just as the horses were being brought out, Harry went to old Nance's cabin and knocked at the door. The prophetess opened the door cautiously. These were alarming times and old Nance looked for wonders everywhere.

"Sho' there. Yo'? Wot you poun' on dat do' for? Wot I dun to ye?"

"I come to bring ye the award."

"The award! Wot fo'? Wot yo' bring me de award fo'? To conjure wi'd?"

"It belongs to Nan. I want you to use it for the

dog. I cannot keep money that I have not earned; not while my word is called in question."

"Sho, you don't say! Maybe yo' ain't so bad as I thought yo' was. A heart that can feel for a dog has some good in it now. Maybe I's wrong. Things are so quare in dis 'ere worl'."

Harry put the guineas into old Nance's hand.

"Sho, wot would de lord say? sho', I'll hab to tell him; sho, now, I'll nebber prophesy agin' ye agin. Yo' just confess dat dar lie yo' tol', and old Nance will never prophesy against ye no mo'. She'll let up on ye and yo' will go over de Jordan singin'."

Harry leaped upon his horse and rode toward the White Post, leaving Greenway Farm in the mellow moonlight that flooded the valley of the Shenandoah.

CHAPTER XIV.

THE VIRGINIA WILD MAN.

A VERY strange event occurred in the Shenandoah Valley at this time, which was just before the French and Indian war. The story in its essential features is quite true, and it is one of the most curious incidents in the early history of our country.

There was an old hunter who made his home in the wilderness where now is Augusta County. One day as he was hunting deer at about the distance of a day's ride from Greenway Court, he saw two eyes gleaming at him from the bushy top of a fallen tree. As deer watch the approach of hunters from thickets, he did not doubt that the eyes were those of a deer.

He raised his rifle and took aim at the eyes of the supposed deer, when something happened that caused him to withhold fire.

The eyes were withdrawn; there was a movement in the fallen tree-top; a head emerged that seemed to be human; then appeared the body of a human being covered with hair.

The hunter was greatly astonished. It was the most curious creature that he had ever seen. There were no apes in the Virginia wilderness. What could it be? The creature approached the hunter. There was blood on his body. The hair on his head was long and shaggy, but he walked erect and seemed intelligent.

He began to make signs and to speak in a strange language. The hunter knew that he must be a human being. The hairy man began to plead with the hunter for help. He could not talk English, but his signs and gestures plainly indicated that he was in great distress and suffering.

The hunter took the strange man to his cabin. He gave him food, which he eagerly devoured; he covered him with clothing and began soon to teach him English words. The man seemed grateful for protection and learned to speak rapidly.

The news that a wild man had been found in the Shenandoah spread through the country and reached Greenway Court. When poor old Nance heard the story she rolled her eyes and told the poor negroes that a man "wid a beast's hide had come up out ob his grabe." She kept her cabin door shut, and so alarmed the little negroes that for a time they did not dare to go away far from the place.

A great hunting-party had been arranged to start

11

from the White Post about this time. Among the
hunters were Mr. Rouzé and Harry Mendell. They
heard the strange story of the wild man at the
Court.

"Let us ride down that way," said Harry. "We
cannot do better than to follow the Blue Ridge on the
west. That course would take us to the place."

The hunting-party were full of curiosity, and when
they left the White Post it was to follow the ridge
toward the west.

They came to the old hunter's cabin and there met
the strange being of which they had heard. They
saw that it was a man of some unknown race, and they
carried back a stirring story to the Court and to their
homes. Old Nance kept the negroes at the Court on
the outlook for wild men and gave to the mystery the
most alarming colorings.

This man's name was Selim. He had been brought
from the north coast of Africa and sold as a slave on
the Mississippi. He was of noble birth, an Algerine,
and a Mohammedan. He had been sent to Constan-
tinople in his youth to be educated. There was hardly
a settler in the Shenandoah Valley more learned than
he. He had been so cruelly treated as a slave that
he ran away and became a wanderer in the woods.
He lived the life of a wild man and reached at last
the great woods of Virginia.

He told the story of his journey toward the rising sun as soon as he could speak English.

He was well clothed when he left the Mississippi. His moccasins soon became worn out and his garments at last were torn and tattered. He used his rags as shoes for his feet. After a time he had neither rags nor shoes. He travelled on alone, naked and eating berries. At times it seemed that he must perish.

The old hunter became a true friend to him. The people who came to see him greatly pitied him when they learned his story. He was carried to Staunton, Va., and there met a Presbyterian minister by the name of Craig whom he claimed to have seen before in a kind of vision.

This clergyman showed him a Greek Testament. The man hugged it to his breast and began to read it. The clergyman resolved to instruct him in Christianity. Selim became a convert, was baptized, and returned to his own country as a missionary.

There he was persecuted, and he came back to Virginia and mingled with accomplished men, who studied Greek literature with him. His portrait, painted by the once-famous artist Peale, may still be seen in Williamsburg.

These were strange, wild days in the Shenandoah Valley. But the old lord, who had been a leader of fashion in London, came to love his new surroundings and seems to have had no wish ever to go beyond the mountains. He had chosen one of the most beautiful spots in the wilderness for a home; settlements were forming all about him; the world was coming to him. Englishmen of rank who came to the colonies made long journeys to see him. So amid his hounds, slaves, and illustrious visitors the years passed. He was a good churchman and seems to have had a Job-like faith.

He was as generous as he was rich. He had a kindly heart for all well-deserving people, and it made him happy to lend them money and give them lands. But he hated dishonor. When once an old Virginian gained a point of law against him by making a man drunk, he refused ever after to speak to him. He himself could never have done such a thing.

The young men of the new country delighted to meet at the White Post, and they pledged their honor in the name of the old lord of Greenway Farm. Harry Mendell came to love the solitary old man, and he felt that his future in life was secure from the hour that he had been taken into his confidence. It was a long ride from Fredericksburg to Winchester, but Harry loved the road that led to the White Post, and the old lord made the Court a home to him, despite the suspicions of the slaves. Harry dreaded old Nance, but it was his inspiration to visit the Court. The holidays often found him there.

CHAPTER XV.

WE are sometimes told in books that Lord Fairfax was a lonely old man. But in few places in the world were there associations of more thrilling events than at the White Post and Greenway Court in his last years.

The most exciting tale ever told at the Court now claims our attention, and, like that of the Virginia wild man, it is true.

There came to the Shenandoah Valley about the time of the French war a rough, untutored boy by the name of Daniel Morgan. He became a farm laborer and lived much at Berryville, near Greenway Court. He was a giant and was proud of his strength, and the towns around the White Post are full of traditions of his wrestlings and feats of daring. He was too rude a lad for better society, and although he must often have been seen about Greenway Court, he could hardly have been a welcome guest there at this period. But he followed the march of Braddock as a wagoner, and his heroism in this campaign won the heart of Washington. When Washington was in Boston at the beginning of the siege, young Daniel Morgan raised a company of riflemen in the towns around the White Post and marched with them across the country to Boston, a distance of some six hundred miles. The young hunters who used to meet at the White Post were of course among them, and so "old Daniel Morgan," as he came to be called, may be numbered among those who in youth were at Greenway Court.

In the year 1758, in the spring, Harry Mendell was sent from Fredericksburg to the forts on the Virginia frontier with a wagon-load of supplies. He went by the way of Winchester and called at Greenway Court, and promised to visit the place again on his return.

One spring afternoon he came riding past the White Post on a horse which he had borrowed at Winchester. Old Nance saw him coming and pulled the bell-rope that rang the alarm-bell on the roof, and ran about the house and cabins, exclaiming, "Dat flying boy!" The negroes ran from the fields and out of the cabins, and the lord and his friends stood on the veranda awaiting the young rider.

He rode into the yard under the great trees.

"What news from the frontier?" asked the lord.

"Strange news, my Lord Fairfax."

"How so?" asked the lord.

"There has been a surprise, and a remarkable thing has happened. They call it at the forts the Ride of the Dead."

At this curious statement old Nance howled, and Nan, the dog, did the same and received patiently the usual cuff on the head.

"You know Morgan?" continued Harry.

"The wagoner?"

"Yes; he who received four hundred and ninety-nine lashes for insulting a British officer and was taken from the tree with his back hanging in shreds."

"A rough fellow, but brave."

"Well, a strange thing has happened to him. A week ago he came riding into one of the forts on a filly and he seemed to be dead. He had been shot."

All were eager to hear the story.

"Give your horse to the groom," said the lord.

"Excuse me, but let me tell it here. I must back to Winchester."

He sat on his horse under the trees. It was near nightfall and all things were touched with the new life of spring.

"I had hardly reached the fort with my wagon," said Harry, "when an alarm was sounded. And there was good cause for it. A strange horse had appeared and on it was a man soaked in blood, and he seemed to be lifeless. His arms were almost buried in the horse's neck. On one side of his cheek was a rough wound and another was on the back of his neck.

"The filly was stopped and stood reeking with foam and with wide nostrils. The animal trembled with fright.

"'Take down the body,' said an officer.

"The form was like that of Morgan, but the face was so besmeared that the men could not say who it was. Water was brought; the surgeon came and bent down and held the man by the wrist.

"'Is he living?' asked the officer.

"'I will tell you in an hour from now,' was the answer.

"They washed his face and threw back the hair.

"'It *is* Morgan,'' said the men.

"'The filly is Morgan's,' said a groom. 'Morgan is dead.'

"My lord, he lay as one dead. After a time the surgeon laid his ear over his heart and said, 'I think he has life.'

"Medicines were given him. The officers gathered around him, and it was told that Morgan had been sent with dispatches to Winchester. The men examined his body.

"'Has he the dispatches still?' asked an officer.

"A search was made and the dispatches were found.

"'Morgan never fails in being true to a trust,' said one of the men.

"They took his body into the fort. It lay there unconscious, but it did not grow cold. We took off his clothing and lifted up the body from the bed. Oh, my lord, it was a terrible sight; the back was covered with scars."

The horse on which Harry sat was restless and interrupted the narrative.

"Is the wagoner living?" asked Lord Fairfax.

"They said that he was living when I left the forts. But he had not spoken."

"Dat dar boy is up to his ole tricks again," said Nance. "We-uns all know Daniel Morgan. He don't ride dead."

"Shut your mouth," said Loveland, the overseer, roughly.

"Have you any letters for Alexandria or Fredericksburg?" asked Harry.

"No, my young friend. But how good it was for you to think of me and to come and ask to do me such favors! May good fortune ride with such as you."

Harry rode away in the long spring twilight over the hills back to Winchester. His story filled the towns around the White Post. Was it true? Would the people ever again see Daniel Morgan alive?

Early in winter a giant rider on a black horse appeared at the White Post. He had ridden down from Winchester. The people gathered around him and asked for his story. He turned down to the Court and was warmly welcomed there. That night he told his story before the great log fire:

"You want to hear my story, good folks, and you could not believe it did you not know it to be true. Whatever I may be—and they say that I am a hard young man—I never yet have practised deception and I never cowered before the face of any man. The lashes that scar my back will testify to that. Then listen to Morgan. His words may not be polite, but know that they are true.

"They chose me to bear secret dispatches to the commander at Winchester. They honored me. The officer said, 'Morgan, you will deliver the dispatches on honor?' and I said, 'I will deliver them or die.' My life was less to me then than those dispatches. Morgan holds that it is more than all things else to have a true heart. Morgan holds that honor is a shining star.

"They gave me two men for an escort. The autumn leaves are now dropping on their graves, and who knows where their graves be? The withering forest covers them somewhere—where I do not know.

"Good folks, listen. You have heard of the Hanging Rocks. The Catawbas and the Delawares fought there. The Rocks overshadow the road.

"We dashed away from the forts, I on my filly and my two comrades on their horses, and rode down to the road that winds under the rocks. The place is not far from the forts and we had little suspicion that a foe was lurking there.

"How beautiful the road was! Morgan loves the forest ways. The streams gushed from the cliffs, the birds were singing, and the woods were still. Not a fern stirred. What was that? Oh, good folks, what followed would make one's heart stand still.

"A rifle-shot flashed from the rocks. Great heavens! what followed that? I saw one of my comrades roll from his horse. There was another report and my other comrade rolled over. A numbness smote me. My mouth filled with blood and my jaw was racked with a terrible pain. I knew that I was shot. Blood was streaming from my neck and face. I thought only of my dispatches. I said, I will save the dispatches!

"The air was rent with the yell of demons. The red devils came leaping down the rocks. I saw them scalp my comrades. I spurred the filly, but the animal quivered and stood trembling.

"An Indian with eyes infernal came running toward me with his scalping-knife in hand. I was streaming with blood, but I thought of the dispatches and spurred the filly again.

"The horse sprang and ran. Ye powers, how that horse ran! I clasped the filly's neck and felt myself whirled through the air. A numbness came over my whole body. I thought it was death. I thought that I was riding with death. I knew that the filly was running for the fort. Were the red demons after me? Were the dispatches safe?

"Horses know. The filly knew. The filly knew that I had lost the rein. The filly knew that I would go to the fort.

"Everything grew dark. I knew that the filly would carry me to the fort now if I could only live; I resolved that the horse should carry me there if I died.

"I clasped the filly's neck as with a death-grasp. If I died my arms should stiffen there. I felt the cool air rush past me; it grew darker; then the world all went and I knew no more.

"But, good folks, Morgan came to himself in the fort. The men were around me. Where had he been?

"'Are the dispatches safe?' I asked.

"'Safe!' said the guard.

"The words were music to Morgan. The dispatches were safe. I had ridden on the wind. I had outridden death and the devils.

"The filly, do you ask? Ah, boys, the filly! The horse knew. A glorious animal is a filly; we will light our pipes on that."

Old Nance thought of Harry's story. She doubted Morgan's. She shook her turban and old Nan howled.

"There are strange things happening here in the wilderness," said my Lord Fairfax.

Nance laid the great oak tables. The fiddles played and hospitalities flowed. Other tales were told, and Morgan mounted his horse late in the evening and rode past the White Post to the farms where he had worked as a wagoner. The episode became a wonder-tale in the towns around the White Post.

CHAPTER XVI.

WASHINGTON'S PERILOUS JOURNEY TO FORT DUQUESNE.

WE now come to one of the most thrilling events of early American history. England and France were at peace at home, when a general war broke out in their great American colonies. The French complaint was that English pioneers persisted in settling in French territory, and the English defence was that the territory thus claimed by the French belonged to England. The scenes of the principal hostilities were settlements on the Ohio River, which formed the present boundary line of the States of Ohio and Virginia. The Monongahela River passes through northern Virginia and flows into the Ohio. The French defences were on the Ohio River, near where the city of Pittsburgh now stands. Take the map of the Middle States and look over the field. France was mistress of the territories north of the Ohio and west of the Mississippi, which last great dominion was known as Louisiana. Canada, or New France, was ruled by a French vice-regal governor. The English colonies were united in purpose and feeling, but had each its own governor, appointed by the Crown.

In 1749 the Governor of New France in Canada sent Colonel de Bienville to define the boundaries of the French territory. His company numbered more than two hundred and embarked upon the St. Lawrence in twenty-three birch-bark canoes. They came to Niagara Falls, carried their canoes on their backs past the great cataract to Chautauqua Lake, and then dropped down the stream to the Ohio and its wonderful and beautiful valley.

As they went along they nailed plates stamped with the arms of France to the trees, and near these plates they buried leaden tablets on which was inscribed "In the name of Louis, King of France."

At Logstown Bienville called a conference of the Indian chiefs and told the council that the English were invading *their* territory and must be driven away. At other places he held councils with the Indians as he sailed down the Ohio to the mouth of the Miami, and he returned to Canada to report that the English settlers were the masters of the Ohio Valley.

The chief of the Miami Indians was called Old Britain. A company was formed in Virginia about 1750 to effect a settlement in the Ohio Valley, and this company concluded a treaty with the Miami chief. The French endeavored to break this treaty. The French concluded their treaties by receiving from the Indians wampum belts as pledges of peace, called "speech belts."

Such was the condition of the two empires in America on the disputed border when the Marquis of Duquesne became Governor and Viceroy of New France and Hon. Robert Dinwiddie the vice-royal acting Governor of Virginia.

Lieutenant-Governor Dinwiddie had no sooner entered upon the duties of his office than he resolved to send an envoy to Marquis Duquesne to protest against the French occupation of the Ohio Valley. Who should this trusty messenger be? He must be a man of courage, culture, and conscience. The burgesses, in answer to this question, answered, *George Washington.* Washington, although only about twenty years of age, accepted the hazardous commission.

The journal kept by Washington during this expedition is full of remarkable incidents and reads like a long story of adventure. It is worthy of the study of every American youth, for it shows the hardy education that prepared him to meet the duties of the Revolution. The spirit which he showed at Princeton and amid the snows of Valley Forge had its first

lessons here.   We give a large part of this journal in
the notes at the end of this story.

He left Williamsburg promptly on the day that he
received his commission to bear the dispatches to the
French commander on the Ohio protesting against
the occupancy of the territory that was allotted to the
English by treaty.   On the 14th of November, 1753,
he reached the extreme frontier of Virginia, accompanied by Mr. Gist, the famous explorer.   Here he
procured guides to conduct him over the Alleghany
Mountains, and pushed on amid storms, perils, and
hardships.   The wilderness was unexplored, the Indian guides were of doubtful fidelity.   The snow
began to fall and severe weather followed the whit-
ening of the earth.

But his return was more perilous than his journey
to the Ohio.   Having delivered the letters from the
Governor of Virginia to the French commander and
received a reply—which was unfavorable—he began
to force his way through the snow toward the Virginia frontier.   His horses became weakened by
fatigue, and he and Mr. Gist were compelled to wander on foot.

Wrapping themselves in their cloaks, which were
their only tents, securing their papers and essential
effects, they faced the stormy wilderness in which
even trails were effaced.   They had not gone far be-

12

fore they fell in with some hostile French Indians, one of whom fired upon them. They took this Indian a prisoner, but sent him on an errand and hurried away while he was gone. Mr. Gist thus relates this story and presents a view of this part of the journey in his journal:

"*Friday, December 7th.*—All encamped at Sugar Creek, five miles from Venango. The creek being very high, we were obliged to carry all our baggage over on trees and swim our horses. The major and I went first over, with our boots on.

"*Monday, December 10th.*—. . . Here we had a creek to cross, very deep; we got over on a tree and got our goods over.

"*Friday, December 21st.*—The ice was so hard we could not break our way through, but were obliged to haul our vessels across a point of land and put them in the creek again. The Indians and three French canoes overtook us here, and the people of one French canoe that was lost, with her cargo of powder and lead. This night we encamped about twenty miles above Venango.

"*Saturday, December 22d.*—Set out. The creek began to be very low, and we were forced to get out to keep our canoe from oversetting several times, the water freezing to our clothes; and we had the pleasure of seeing the French overset and the brandy and wine floating in the creek, and run by them and left them to shift for themselves.

"*Thursday, December 27th.*—We rose early in the morning and set out about 2 o'clock. Got to the Murthering town, on the southeast fork of Beacon Creek. Here we met an Indian, whom I thought I had seen at Joncaire's, at Venango, when on our journey up to the French fort. This fellow called me by my Indian name and pretended to be very glad to see me. He asked me several questions, as how we came to travel on foot, when we left Venango, where we parted with our horses, and when they would be there, etc. Major Washington insisted on travelling on the nearest way to the forks of the Alleghany. We asked the Indian if he could go with us and show us the nearest way. The Indian seemed very glad and ready to go. Upon which we set out, and the Indian took the major's pack. We travelled very brisk for eight or ten miles, when the major's feet grew very sore and he very weary, and the Indian steered too much northeastwardly. The major [Washington] desired to encamp, to which the Indian asked to carry his gun. But he refused that, and the Indian grew churlish and pressed us to keep on, telling us that there were Ottawa Indians in the woods, and they would scalp us if we lay out, but go to his cabin and we should be safe. I thought very ill of

the fellow, but did not care to let the major know I
mistrusted him. But he soon mistrusted him as much
as I. He said he could hear a gun to his cabin, and
steered us more northwardly. We grew uneasy, and
then he said two whoops might be heard to his cabin.
We went two miles further; then the major said
he would stay at the next water. But before we came
to water we came to a clear meadow; it was very
light and snow on the ground. The Indian made a
stop, turned about; the major saw him point his gun
toward us and fire; said the major, 'Are you shot?'
'No,' said I. Upon which the Indian ran forward to
a big standing white oak, but we were soon with him.
I would have killed him, but the major would not
suffer me to kill him. We let him charge his gun;
we found he put in a ball; then we took care of him.
The major or I always stood by the guns; we made
him make a fire for us by a little run, as if we intended to sleep there. I said to the major, 'As you
will not have him killed, we must get him away, and
then we must travel all night.' Upon which I said
to the Indian, 'I suppose you were lost and fired
your gun.' He said he knew the way to his cabin,
and 'twas but a little way. 'Well,' said I, 'do you
go home; and as we are much tired, we will follow
your track in the morning.' He was glad to get away.
I followed him and listened until he was fairly out of

Gist saves Washington from drowning.

the way, and then we set out about half a mile, when we made a fire, set our compass and fixed our course, and travelled all night, and in the morning we were on the head of Piney Creek.

"*Saturday, December 29th.*—. . . The major having fallen in from off the raft, and my fingers frost-bitten, and the sun down, and very cold, we contented ourselves encamped upon that island. It was deep water between us and the shore; but the cold did us some service, for in the morning it was frozen hard enough for us to pass over on the ice."

The next day they came to a river, which they found frozen far from the shore, but with an open channel.

"We must build a raft," said Washington.

"We have only a hatchet with which to do it," answered Gist.

"That must answer our purpose. There is no time to lose."

The timber was cut and the raft was made.

When they were half over the river on the raft, the current bore down the drift of broken ice upon them and they were in danger of drowning.

Washington put out his rude oar or steering-pole to stop the raft, that the ice might drift by, when he was suddenly thrown into deep water, and saved himself only by catching hold of one of the logs. He

suffered severely from the chill. Mr. Gist had his
hands and feet frozen, and they were only kept from
perishing by resolution. They reached Williamsburg
on January 16th, 1754. The dispatches showed that
the French denied the English claim to the Ohio
Valley.

The story of Washington and Gist on the raft became a wonder-tale in Virginia. Gist once, and perhaps twice, saved Washington from drowning. The
adventurous journey gave to young Washington the
reputation of possessing courage that was equal to
any event. This reputation was sustained by a
declaration which he made when the Indian tribes
became hostile to the Virginia pioneers after Braddock's defeat, of which we shall give some account:

" *The supplicating tears of the women and moving petitions of the men melt me with such deadly sorrow that I
solemnly declare, if I know my own mind, I could offer
myself a willing sacrifice to the butchering enemy provided
that would contribute to the people's ease.*"

His disregard of bullets at the conflict in which
Braddock, of which we are to relate the story, fell
had proven this declaration to be most sincere. He
was ready to offer all that he had to the cause of his
country, and he feared nothing but dishonor.

From youth to age he believed that he who made
duty the purpose of his life would be divinely guided.

He walked by faith, like men who believed in commissions from the skies. Says an eloquent writer, who clearly saw the mould and motives of his character formed in youth in the wilderness in perilous times, and who summed up his virtues after his death:

"With a midshipman's commission in his pocket and his baggage on board the vessel, a voice whispered, 'Honor thy mother.' His inclination was for the voyage, but duty to his mother changed his purpose. During his brother Augustine's illness he was devising the best means to cheer and comfort him. At times he would sit and read to him hour after hour. And when his coughing spasms occurred, he would hold his drooping head, and wipe the cold sweat from his brow, and administer to his every want with all the patience of a Christian. When very young, Washington would listen to a father's instruction, and sit hours listening with delight to the discourses of a father on the wisdom, perfection, and glory of the Deity as displayed in the harmonious works of nature, and thus prepared for conceiving the sublime truths of revelation. He was frequently known on the Sabbath to read the Scriptures and pray with the regiment when the chaplain of the army was absent. One of his aids in the French war, when on a visit to his marquee, says he often found him kneeling in prayer. Rev. Mr. Lee Massy, a rector of Washington's parish, says 'he never knew so constant an attendant at church,' and that his reverence while present greatly aided him in his ministry. At his table, surrounded with guests, he did not forget to thank the Giver of all blessings.

"Judge Harrison, his secretary, says that 'whenever the general could be spared from the camp on the Sabbath, he never failed riding out to some neighboring church, to join those who were in public worshipping the great Creator.' When the Americans had been fired on by the British and several of the Americans were killed, he was heard to say: 'I grieve for the death of my countrymen, but rejoice that the British are determined to keep God on our side.' He uttered the sentiment recorded in several manuscripts of his own writing, that 'the smiles of Heaven can never be expected on a nation that disregards the eternal rules of order and right which Heaven itself has ordained.'

"When chosen President of the United States by the unanimous voice of the people, in reply to the grateful acknowledgments of Congress for his past services, he says: 'When I contemplate the interposition of Providence, which was visibly manifested in guiding us through the Revolution, in preparing us for the reception of the general government, and in conciliating the good will of the people of America toward one another after its adoption, I feel myself oppressed and almost *overwhelmed with a sense of the Divine munificence.*   I feel that nothing is due to my personal agency in all those complicated and wonderful events, except what can simply be attributed to the exertions of an honest zeal for the good of my country.' "

This character was formed by the self-discipline of youth.   He who would govern others must learn to master himself, and only such a young man can fulfil the largest gifts that are in him.

CHAPTER XVII.

STIRRING events were at hand. Harry heard of them through Mr. Rouzé and again and again asked:

"If there should be a war will there be couriers from Boston?"

"Likely," said Mr. Rouzé. "The burgesses are in correspondence with ex-Governor Shirley, the colonial agent of Massachusetts."

The Southern colonies were arming to defend the English cause in the valley of the Ohio. A struggle for the continent was impending. Should the English cross or the French *fleur-de-lis* possess the vast empire of the lakes and rivers? To form an army for the protection of the English settlers on the Ohio and its arms, North Carolina raised some four hundred men, Virginia some three hundred. Two companies of English soldiers came from New York and one from South Carolina. The major of the Virginia company was young George Washington.

While preparation for war was thus going on, the

French, to bar the passage of the English down the Ohio, built a strong fort near where Pittsburgh now stands, which they named Fort Duquesne.

Washington with a company of Virginians advanced from Alexandria to Wills Creek and into the wilderness. He there encountered a scouting French force; a slight battle followed and Washington drew back, but this shedding of blood by organized forces set England, France, and their American colonies on fire. The French and Indian war for the valley of the Ohio was at hand. Washington was promoted to the command of a Virginia regiment, and his own military career thus began.

In the early winter of 1755 England sent Major-General Braddock with two regiments, each five hundred strong, to Virginia. Braddock was a proud, self-sufficient man, but brave, gallant, and educated in the European arts of war.

On arriving in Virginia he assumed a haughty bearing and laughed at the Virginia militia. He commanded the Virginian troops to be drilled after the English manner; to move in solid bodies in picturesque motions, to wheel as before a tactician, and to practise and manœuvre like the home army in camp.

George Washington had earned a place as a regimental commander, but General Braddock resolved to assume the whole responsibility of the campaign.

"Will you accept a place on my staff as *aide-de-camp?*" asked Braddock of the young Virginia officer.

It must have hurt young Washington's pride to have accepted the position, but he answered as should a soldier loyal to a cause:

"Yes, at your service wherever the cause demands my sword."

When young Washington rode out to see the English tactics taught to some Virginia militia he would say:

"That will not do here."

"Why?" would ask the English officer.

"This is forest fighting."

"And what is that?"

"To be effective one must fight his own way—his skill must be individual. Our Indian enemies fight behind trees and in ambush. We must meet them in no vain parades, but in a way that will make every shot tell."

The army moved toward the Ohio in early summer. "One of the most beautiful sights," said Washington, "that I ever saw," at the last period of the march. The English soldiers were a fine body of men, in full equipment. The officers had no doubt of success, of easy victory, and a glorious return.

The headquarters of General Braddock was at Alexandria, Va. From here he marched to Win-

chester and is supposed to have visited Greenway
Court. The forming of the new English and provincial army brought to the Northern Neck a gallant soldier from Massachusetts, William Shirley.
He was a son of William Shirley, ex-Governor of
Massachusetts. The latter had lived in the Province
House, was the builder of a beautiful private estate,
now known as the Eustis place, died some years
later and was buried in the King's Chapel, Boston,
and his coat of arms may still be seen in pictures
and in antiquarian rooms.

Young William Shirley became an intimate friend
of George Washington, and the two, like all the English and provincial officers, were made welcome to
the hospitalities of Greenway Court.

Harry Mendell saw the gallant young soldier there
in company with Washington. He knew that the
father of the young man had sent the courier from
Boston to Virginia who had met his mother in her
wanderings when the horseshoe was mysteriously
found. He had a strong desire to speak with him
and to ask him if he knew the name of this courier.
But the superior bearing of the young man caused
him to hesitate. Young Shirley was held in admira-
tion by every one, for he was already famous as a
soldier.

There came at last an opportunity for Harry to

approach the young officer as he was resting one day from a ride in the shadows of the trees of the Court.

"May I address you, sir?" he said, almost timidly.

"Yes, my boy. What have you to say to me? Are you one of the boys of Greenway Court?"

"I can hardly claim that honor, sir. I wish I were, sir, for the lord has been very good to me. There is a matter, sir, in which you might be able to do me a favor. Your father was Governor of Massachusetts, sir?"

"Yes, my boy, and is now military commissioner."

"He sent a courier from Boston to Virginia two years ago. That courier met my mother on the Potomac. Can you tell me who that courier was?"

"No, my boy, I have been much away from my father in the military service. Why do you wish to know?"

"My mother is now dead. That courier from Boston had a conversation with her about a matter that is of great interest to me. She tried to tell me about it just before she died, but her mind wandered and her strength failed."

"I would be glad to do you any service, my boy. Speak to me again about the matter, and I will give you a note to my father and he will answer your question."

"You are very kind, sir."

"Not at all, my boy."

He bowed with a generous expression. How noble he looked! He turned his horse to meet William Fairfax, and the two sat on their horses and talked together under the great still trees.

Harry was to accompany the Virginia division of the army on the campaign as a messenger. He was delighted when he learned that his duties would bring him into association with George Washington and William Shirley.

It was a sad day for Virginia when the army left Alexandria. The officers were full of hope, but most of them were never to return again.

It was amid the green forests of the beautiful Virginia May and June that the army marched from the Potomac on their slow way toward the great Ohio Valley.

The people of the Shenandoah Valley assembled at Winchester to see the army pass by. Braddock rode in state coach like a king. He wore a brilliant uniform, and his sash, which was of strong silk, was large enough for a hammock.

Old Nance was in the street and saw his coach depart. It is safe to prophesy along the line of unfailing principles of life. She had been told that "pride goes before destruction and a haughty spirit before a fall," and when she saw the flowing sash she said:

"Look at him now. That sash will be bloody before he ever comes back."

She was right. That sash was to have a history. They passed over the Alleghanies and through the cool shadows of grand forests with light hearts and flying colors, and often with gay music and rolling of drums.

On the march Harry often was summoned to do errands for William Shirley. The gentlemanly bearing of this young officer had something under it more than form. He had a warm heart and a kindliness that won Harry's affection. It became the boy's happiness to receive an order from him and to execute it in his best and most expeditious way.

Once on the march an incident occurred that made Harry's affectionate regard for the gallant William Shirley glow into an inspiration. The young officer had been told Harry's curious history by some one, perhaps by Washington or himself.

"You have had some trouble, I understand, and you wish to make your honor clear," said the young officer.

"Yes," answered Harry.

"You have been injured, but you will rise above it, and those who have doubted you will come to believe in your sincerity. The scales of Time weigh true."

Harry drew his rein.

"Sir, your words are like a message from Heaven to me. I cannot help the accidents of the past, but, sir——"

The young officer drew his rein and looked the manly boy full in the face.

"Sir," continued Harry, "I intend so to live that he who seeks to injure me will only belittle himself."

The young officer lifted his hat.

"And, Harry Mendell, I will be your friend. You are a poor boy, as I learn. But honor is more than knighthood."

On the 7th of July the army had arrived within eight miles of the French fort. The officers felt sure of a splendid engagement and the triumphs of skilled arms, of winning Fort Duquesne in four days, as Braddock had told them, and of "other victories."

Only Washington, the provincial aide, was not so confident. "Beware of ambush," he said to General Braddock, and he again and again repeated the warning: "Beware of ambush."

Ambush? What was that? What were the wiles of unorganized savages to this glittering, disciplined host, whose proud commander's will was law?

Before them now rose a hard country, in which were a ford and a narrow defile.

The army crossed the ford of the Monongahela for

13

its final march.   They had left behind the sick soldiers as well as the horses that had become weak for
want of forage.   Light horsemen led the way, followed by a fine column of soldiers under the English
General Gage, afterward of revolutionary fame and a
commander at Boston at the time of the early scenes
of the Revolutionary War.   The English regiments
and the provincials followed, with artillery, wagons,
and flanking parties.

They were marching through a defile of green
trees, when an alarm was given.   The guides of the
two armies had seen each other.

But hark—

What was that?

The forest rang with a piercing cry as though
the trees had gone mad.   What was happening?
There were flashings of muskets in unseen hands,
and English soldiers were falling as though smitten
by foes in the air.   The English guns thundered.
There was a brief silence.   The English army rushed
forward cheering, when the green forest seemed to
turn into swarms of savages on every hand.   The air
rained death.   What was the use of skilled warfare
now?   "Beware of ambush!"

War-whoop after war-whoop rose.   The English
officers had never dreamed of an event like this.
They were bewildered; the soldiers found themselves

merely targets standing in solid columns to be shot down.

Braddock rushed to the support of his officers. What a sight met his eyes!

The advance English soldiers were already in full retreat, having left their cannon. The forest field was strewn with dead and dying. Every trunk of a tree seemed to be a little fortress for some copper-colored foe, and the air was still raining death. The flying soldiers became mixed with the advancing column, and any systematic warfare would have been almost as useless as a war with the air.

The Virginians whom Braddock had ridiculed now came forward, and they began to meet the foe single-handed and checked the fury of the Indian attack.

When Braddock saw the Virginians fighting behind trees, his pride of military education rose again. He uttered a fearful oath and ordered:

"Form into line!"

The Virginians did not all obey. Seeing some of them still fighting behind trunks of trees, he attempted to beat them back with the flat of his own sword.

"Provincials, form into line!"

They could not obey.

Braddock was as brave as he was obstinate; he rushed hither and thither, issuing commands.

But where was the foe? He heard fearful yells, saw the puffs of smoke and the hail of deadly weapons, but no foe was to be seen. The trees seemed to have turned into giant warriors and to pour from their hearts the fires and poison of destruction. It was like a forest at war.

The horses became wild and added to the confusion. Braddock's horse fell dead, but he mounted another; that fell dead, but he leaped upon another, and that fell dead. Washington had two horses shot under him.

In the thick of the battle Washington implored him to let his men break ranks.

"Does a Virginia colonel presume to tell an English general how to fight?" he answered haughtily.

Gage was wounded; of eighty-six officers, more than sixty fell dead, dying, or wounded. The common soldiers had fallen, or were falling, like reeds in the river winds.

In the midst of the slaughter the haughty spirit of Braddock never faltered.

"Let no provincial hide himself behind a tree," he said.

Thomas Faucett, a provincial soldier, disobeyed. Braddock saw him sheltering himself behind a tree after the Indian manner, and he rode up to him and struck him with his sword. The brother of Faucett saw the act and fired upon his chief. The proud man wheeled, with an awful look in his face. Suddenly he reeled on his horse. The shot had struck him, entering his lungs. He rolled to the ground.

"Leave me where I lie," he said bravely. Two Virginians took up his agonized body and bore it to the rear.

The army now were in full retreat and rushing in disorder over the ford that they had passed so gayly and proudly.

Young Washington and the Virginia and provincial troops had alone acted wisely. "The Virginia colonel," as Braddock had contemptuously called him, became the natural leader of the provincial troops, who checked the enemy and covered the retreat.

They took from Braddock his silk sash and laid him in it as in a hammock. They lifted him up in it between the saddles of two horses and bore him away. They came at last to a place near Fort Necessity, or Great Meadows.

"Who would have thought it? Who would have thought it?" exclaimed Braddock as he reviewed the defeat.

That sash was indeed bloody before they laid him down to die.

Harry Mendell? Washington had fallen sick on the outward march, and he had served him with his

best care. He had loved to ride as near William
Shirley as possible when the soldiers marched at will.
He crossed the river at young Shirley's side.

"I will give you that letter when we return," the
young officer said to him just before the war-whoop
from the unseen foe smote the air. But the gallant
Shirley never returned. He fell on the field and
never saw the foe.

Harry never left Washington in the thick fight.
He was at Washington's s... ~, waiting the aide's commands, when the two horses were shot. He was twice
slightly wounded, and his own horse was shot. He
felt no fear; he only thought of duty. He was "true
to the best that was in him." Washington saw it
and remembered it.

Three days after Braddock was wounded he died in
the forest attended by Washington's provincials.

That was a solemn hour of night when George
Washington read over the body of Braddock the
Episcopal burial service 'neath the moon and stars:
"I am the resurrection and the life." The forest
was dark and torches flared over the yet darker
grave. They buried Braddock in the road, that
the Indians might not discover and mutilate his
body, and the Virginians that returned bore heavy
news of the battle of the Monongahela to Greenway
Court. But Washington came back a hero in the

eyes of the province, and Harry a hero in Washington's eyes.

Harry Mendell returned to Mr. Rouzé's. The family of his benefactor had become large, and they were very poor. Harry served him as a son.

One dream now began to haunt his life. It was that he might go to Boston and meet Governor Shirley and tell him of his son's promise, and learn who was the mysterious courier from Boston who had met his mother, for he tried in vain to learn the name from the Governor of Virginia and the burgesses. They only knew that the man came from Governor Shirley and was the "courier from Boston."

Harry began to cherish a secret purpose to seek to become an official courier or dispatch-bearer between the provinces. Could he secure such a commission? Would the burgesses trust him?

CHAPTER XVIII.

HARRY BECOMES A COURIER.

THERE were two persons who never lost an opportunity to ridicule Harry's story of his unwilling ride: the negro woman Nance and the overseer Loveland. Neither was a wholly desirable character among the merry, hospitable household of Greenway Court. But Nance, although she had an unamiable and suspicious disposition, was an example of hard and faithful work to the slaves. Her "fists," as she expressed her peculiar qualifications, were "full of days' work." Mr. Loveland, though disliked as an evil-speaking man, a spy, and informer, was yet a natural and methodical organizer and was accurate and thorough in his work. Both had made themselves so useful to the old lord that he felt that he could trust them as few others for certain responsible services, and so he retained them and bore with them, checking them when their tendencies were likely to end in injustice to others.

A party of young hunters were among the "boys

of Greenway Court." They used to assemble there
in the red autumns, with fine horses and baying
hounds, and follow the old lord to the chase of the
fox and deer. The sons of English nobles were
sometimes found in the old Virginia hunting-parties,
and such were sure to find a warm welcome at Greenway Court.

Harry was a swift and sure rider, one of the best
of the young Virginian horsemen, notwithstanding
his unfavorable introduction to the Court through
the wilful mare.

One morning as a hunting-party was gathering at
the Court, Lord Fairfax and Mr. Loveland stood on
the veranda, and Harry was seated on a fine horse
in the yard. The old negress, having already "done
work enough for two" for a whole day, as she flat-
tered herself, was walking to and fro, her turban
lightly tossing about like a queen's and her arms
swinging backward and forward in a most self-sufficient and decisive manner. A few of the young
hunters had already gathered in the yard.

"My boy," said Lord Fairfax, "you ride well.
You are a natural rider. You *ought* to be a courier.
You might then some time meet the 'courier from
Boston.'"

"Yes," said Mr. Loveland to Harry, "a fine courier
you would make. You could cross rivers without

bridges. You could give the horse's ear a twist and whoop, ha, and he would mount up into the air and fly like one of the wild geese. You would beat one of the horses we read about in the 'Arabian Nights.'"

Old Nance had stopped and caught the spirit of what the overseer was saying. "Dat so, dat so," she said, bowing over. "But wot if he could cunjure, and set the horse a-flying among the stars, if he couldn't guide him at all, no mor'n the gale o' winds? What den? You think ole Nance don't know nothin' at all, 'cos o' her color. But ole Nance can see. Dat boy a *cour'er!* Start fo' de east and ride to de wes'; pull his rein fo' de nof' and go to de souf'; set out fo' Ameriky and get to Afriky. Suppose de hoss could be cunjured to walk upon de water? What good dat do if he was sure to go de *wrong* way?"

"Yes," said the overseer, "he would be a great courier. He would have news to tell. He could spin dispatches in the air. He would do to ride between Williamsburg and Philadelphia and Boston. He would have news to tell that would set the bells to ringing:"

"He would see armies in visions ob de night," said old Nance, bending her turban and shaking her head. "He would carry messages to the king."

"Wouldn't need any ships, would he, Nance?" said

the overseer. "That boy will be crazy long before the age his mother began to lose her wits."

"Loveland," said the lord, "you are dealing with things that can't be helped. Hurt no one's feelings without a cause. The boy rides well."

"Courier!" Harry's spirit had bounded at the word. He had been dreaming of it. He had seen what the office of courier was in connection with the preparations for the campaign against Braddock. He had seen the messengers of the high-spirited general flying hither and thither—from Williamsburg to the Carolinas, and to Fredericksburg, Alexandria, and Winchester. "Courier!" The word inspired him, and the words, "You ride well," filled him with pride.

"Crazy!" His heart sank at the word. He thought of his poor mother and her "spells," as her clouded days were called. Would he ever suffer her misfortune? And was he really in his right mind when he thought the horse walked over the river on the water?

The young hunters had laughed at the opinions of old Nance. Their laugh had cut him to the quick.

"The courier from Boston!" That thought from this hour took possession of his mind more and more. Were he to find the postman from Boston to whom allusion had been made, would not that courier be able to tell him some strange story as to where and how the horseshoe had been found? He asked this question daily.

The hope of some time and somehow meeting the courier from Boston came to form a kind of rainbow in the clouds of his mind. Old Nance seemed to guess the new hope, and as he rode away she passed by the horse and lifted her finger and shook it in the air.

"Don't ye never think that no postman from Boston is ebber gwine to tell you how a horse cast a shoe walking on the water. Boy, your head is loose, just like yees mother's. Ole Nance knows."

Harry's feelings fell again. He knew that old Nance expressed a lurking opinion held by many. But he overheard a remark that day, after he had done some splendid riding for a hunting-party, which wounded his feelings more deeply than the heedless allusions that had been so cruelly made regarding the helpless condition of his mother.

"That boy does ride finely," said a young military officer to Lord Fairfax. "He would be a fine courier for the new campaign, *but could he be trusted?*"

"That remains to be seen," said Lord Fairfax.

As the hunting-party were returning in the shadows of the blazing autumn twilight Harry said to Mr. Rouzé, "You do not know how I suffer at times. I suffer nights; I think and think, until my heart beats so that it shakes the bed."

"Do your best and all will be well at the end."

"Mr. Rouzé, no one can do his best or be the best that is in him except he have virtue and honor, as Lord Fairfax says. But to be suspected of dishonor by such men as these, when one has nothing but his own sense of right, is hard to bear. Mr. Rouzé, what is to become of me? I sometimes wish that I were dead. I can't help it."

"Harry, time tells the truth about all things and all men at last. Harry, be more noble than any of us. Trust God and *fight* for the highest character. These dark days will make you a strong man. They will mould your habits and make your integrity like a rock. Misfortunes are to a right-minded man his best friends. The law of moral growth is resistance, as Lord Fairfax says. Harry, mark my words: You will one day be as greatly honored by the confidence of men as you are now suspected and slighted. Don't be a coward! Fight, wait, and trust!"

"I *will*, Mr. Rouzé."

"And some day you will be a blessing to me."

"Heaven answer that prayer, Mr. Rouzé. If that should ever happen, the day will be a happy one to Harry Mendell."

Tears filled the boy's eyes. He was tender-hearted,

and a sense of his wrongs often led him to brood over his strange lot, and his sore heart found relief only in tears. But they were not weak tears.

The defeat of Braddock and the honors won by Washington and the Virginians aroused the Southern colonies to make new efforts to wrest the region of the lakes and the Ohio Valley from the French. To this purpose the old Baron of Cameron was alive, and he called into his counsel and enterprise the boys of Greenway Court. He resolved to help arm and equip a body of young horsemen for the service, and the court-yard was for a time full of cavaliers and blooded horses, eager to retrieve the disgrace that had fallen to the English provincial army.

What a scene must Greenway Court have presented on the mornings when the young cavalrymen came to pay their respects to the old baron! Young Washington was there. Beside him may have stood Richard Henry Lee, who was born in 1732 and so was about Washington's age. Who would then have thought that this same Richard Henry Lee would one day offer a resolution to the provincial Congress that the "United Colonies are and of a right ought to be free and independent States?"

Arthur Lee may have been there, then a boy. Francis Lightfoot Lee and the other brothers of Richard Henry Lee, all of them to become famous in the halls of state as the friends of freedom, were likely to have been there. So, also, were Mr. Gist, the explorer and mountaineer, and the friendly Indian warriors, with their gay plumes. Here at times came officers from England and descendants from the early settlers of Jamestown.

The mountainous forest roads rang with horses' feet and the baying of hounds. Old Lord Fairfax was full of ardor to overthrow the French rule in the region of the rivers and lakes. He was a stanch royalist, and he could not have dreamed that the young men whom he was inspiring and training would one day wrest not only an empire from France, but the United Colonies from the crown of the English king!

When young Washington again led the gallant Virginians to the valley of the Ohio the march was one of peace. Washington seemed destined to be a man of defeats that end in victory, and so it was in the French War. The French abandoned the lake and river country and left the Ohio and inland seas to the English. The city of Pittsburgh has slowly arisen on the spot where Fort Duquesne and its defences stood. The French empire fell with Montcalm in Canada on the Plains of Abraham, 1759.

The heroism of Harry Mendell at the battle of the Monongahela had won the affection of both young

Washington and the old baron. The strange story that Harry had told in regard to crossing the Potomac was not yet clear, but no one now except Loveland and black Nance doubted the heroism of his soul.

"Harry Mendell," said the colonel of the Fairfax light horsemen one day, "at the request of Lord Fairfax I appoint you courier and confidential dispatch-bearer to our new expeditions. Lord Fairfax says that you have honor, and he has given you a chance to show it."

"He can fly just like a bat in the night," said Loveland, who was in hearing. "Be careful that you are not minus a horse some day."

Harry was sent to Quebec in that final campaign in which Wolfe fell in the hour of victory.

One evening in the autumn of that eventful year he suddenly appeared at Greenway Court several days before he was expected. Old Nance first saw him coming and she rang the bell and ran into the manor-house crying:

"Signs and wonders! Moses and de 'postles, ole Nance has had a vision. Wot ye think I's don' see now?"

The old lord met her intrusion with a kindly reproving look.

"What has happened, Nance?"

"Signs and wonders! That *cunjured* boy——"

"Where?"

"He has come down from the skies."

"Where?"

"Leaped ober de ribbers and de oceans——"

"Where?"

"*There!*"

A clatter of hoofs brought Lord Fairfax to the veranda.

"Quebec has fallen, my lord," Harry said. "But Wolfe is dead."

Harry took supper again that night in the farmhouse, and the old baron seemed grateful to entertain him as before. He described the scene of the battle: how Wolfe gained the fortress by the night surprise. They talked long and late. The white turban of old Nance was at times seen at the windows. She was in great distress and ran from the house to the cabins crying, "Pots and kettles! Needles and pins! Wot Massa Fairfax doin' agin 'long wid that flying boy?"

The two sat up late together by the great fire.

Harry related how that as Wolfe had crossed the river before the fortress he had repeated a poem called "Gray's Elegy."

"I have little education, my lord," said Harry, "and I have few books. I heard an officer repeat part of the poem. His words began:

14

"'Nor you, ye proud, impute—' I wish I might hear it again."

"I love that poem and can repeat the extract," said Lord Fairfax. "Was it not this?

"'Nor you, ye proud, impute to these the fault,
   If Mem'ry o'er their tomb no trophies raise,
  Where, thro' the long-drawn aisle and fretted vault,
   The pealing anthem swells the note of praise.'"

He then repeated much of the poem.

Harry sat silent and drank in the solemn melody of the thought and expression. The old baron did not speak again for some minutes after he had concluded.

The fire blazed on the hearth, the watch-dogs lay beside it, and the white turban of old Nance bobbed before the window. Harry to her had become a kind of wizard. Suddenly Harry started up and said:

"I must start to-night for Williamsburg to surrender my commission. I have only slept on horseback for three nights. But I must not lose an hour."

Old Nance heard him speak of sleeping on horseback and fled to the cabins in the greatest terror.

"Shut your doors and fasten the windows," said she to the slaves. "The cunjured boy is comin' out, and as sure's you're born he's goin' to fly!"

She watched Harry from the door and saw him mount a new horse and fly swiftly away.

"He's flown," she said. "I's seen 'im mountin' up into the air, an he's left behin' the hill. Wot will happen next, hebben only knows. Dese be de las' times!"

The cool winds came from the mountains of pines. Nance breathed them as a tonic, and amid waking visions and dreams she returned to her rest, saying, "Signs and wonders! Signs and wonders!"

What may have been the thoughts of the old Baron of Cameron as to the trend of the events of the time we cannot tell. The French empire had fallen. The English colonies were becoming restless for larger freedom. Strange ideas were in the air. There was a growing discontent among the colonies with the severe rule of the English crown. America was dreaming her first thought of liberty, which in English eyes was treason.

CHAPTER XIX.

A CRISIS.

MR. ROUZÉ owned a large tract of land which he had secured under the colonial charter, but he was yet very poor. His family had grown from two to seven, not including Harry. Five children played around his log-cabin door. He relied upon Harry for help in all emergencies. He was not able to buy or even to hire slaves. Harry worked for his benefactor like a son.

The income from his estate failed to pay the expenses of his family. He became at times greatly depressed in spirits, but on such days he appeared to others to be very lively, witty, and unconcerned. He would sing old English songs and whistle provincial tunes, but when alone would sit down upon a log and, holding his chin in his hands, would stare into the vacant air. When in these moods, if he saw one of his children, his eyes would fill with tears and he would say, "I don't mind myself; no matter what becomes of me; but *they?*"

In one of these times of mental depression George Washington came riding down the road to the Northern Neck from Fredericksburg. He reined his horse before the logs that Mr. Rouzé used for seats under the noble trees before his cabin door. Mr. Rouzé was sitting in the shade alone in deep reverie, and did not notice the young officer until a voice aroused him.

"I beg your pardon, Mr. Rouzé, I do not like to break in upon your thoughts if they are agreeable ones, which I hope they are. A man with your nature deserves to be happy. I hope you are well."

"*Colonel* Washington [using the common title], you speak me kindly. I am well, I thank you; but how can a man with a growing family be happy when every year finds him deeper and deeper in debt?"

"My friend, you have my sympathy as you have my respect, for you are a whole-souled man and industrious. There is no man in Virginia who merits prosperity more than you. Have you that boy with you yet?"

"Harry Mendell?"

"Yes, that was his name."

"Yes, and he is a son to me."

"You have cleared his character by proving his strange story to be true?"

"Yes, there is not the faintest suspicion in most

minds that rests on his character now. But he himself is not satisfied. He wants to find the 'courier
from Boston.' But that is not here nor there. He
is a boy of honor. A more truthful boy I never
knew. I am glad for all that I did for him."

"Mr. Rouzé, he is a brave lad, as I have seen, and
there are few men who would have done as much for
a stranger. I never knew so unlikely a story that
was proven to be true. I shall always hold your
memory and that of the boy in the highest respect."

"Colonel Washington, I have been thinking of ask-
ing a favor of you, but it hurts my spirit to do it.
I am in trouble, and I do not know in which way to
turn. When I sit down to rest after my day's work
and begin to think my heart sinks within me like
lead."

"Ask any favor, my friend. I shall hear it with
willing ears and an open heart. I shall grant it if it
seems to me reasonable and it be within my power."

"Colonel Washington, if I could secure a loan of
two hundred pounds, I would be a happy man.
Would *you* lend me that amount for ten years? These
hands shall be browned and these feet ache with
toil to pay the debt. I would not ask it for myself;
but I often work fourteen hours a day, and my wife
and children need clothes and food, and I cannot
bear to see them suffer. I pay Harry nothing for his

labor. The boy works for me out of love and gratitude."

"You need not apologize, my friend. You have a
free nature, but you do your best. I will think of your
request."

The young officer was about to draw the rein, when
Harry Mendell appeared, and with uncovered head
stood beside Mr. Rouzé.

"My boy, you found a friend in Mr. Rouzé."

"Sir, there can be no better friend in the world.
I owe my good name to him. May *he* never want a
friend!"

"He shall not, my boy, while I live and his heart is
true."

There was a silence. The long summer shadows
fell across the way. The crimson light of the west
was mingled with the green leaves of the trees. A
cardinal bird flashed here and there amid the twilight stillness of the forest.

Washington gazed earnestly on the forester and
the boy.

"Mr. Rouzé!"

"My good neighbor?"

"You shall not want for a friend. I *will* loan you
two hundred pounds for ten years, and for your sake
I hope that you will be able to pay it when it becomes
due, and that you may live to possess many times

that sum.   Come to Mount Vernon on any day and you shall have the money."

He bowed and rode away down the cool, shaded road.   Mr. Rouzé sat down and covered his face with his hands.

"Harry, my boy, that loan will make me an independent man.   I can build a home now, and cribs, and buy seeds for another year.   A new birthday of life will begin.   Harry, it was you that did it—*you.*"

"No, Mr. Rouzé, it was what you did for me.   It is no common thing to have a friend in George Washington.   He is a silent man, but his heart is true.   He is a man's friend under all circumstances, they say."

"Yes, Harry, a friend for all weathers, and he will be your friend while you keep your honor."

"And yours."

"But, Harry, we cannot tell what may happen. This is a new country and there are likely to come uncertain times again.   Suppose I should not be able to pay the two hundred pounds in ten years?"

"I should hope that I might be able to pay it for you.   All that I ever may be or have shall be at your service."

"If I have not money, Harry, I do have *hearts.* Even old Lord Fairfax speaks in an affectionate manner when he talks to me.   I can feel the atmosphere of his kindly influence. I hope Heaven will help me discharge this debt like a man."

"Washington will never push you for the debt so as to bring you into trouble or dishonor."

"No, Harry, not he! But this is a changeable world, and neither he nor I can tell what may happen. But I would rather be a debtor to George Washington than to any other man."

"Mr. Rouzé, there are some hearts that cannot be untrue. You can trust the heart of Washington."

"Yes, my boy, I thank Heaven that there are some hearts that we can trust, and that the heart of Washington is one of them."

The period between the French and Indian war and the Revolution was one of the most generous and prosperous in Virginia history. The "F. F. V.," as the first families in Virginia came to be known, lived almost in a style of the feudal age in England. They had immense estates, of which the barony of Lord Fairfax with its millions of acres was the largest; retinues of servants, mostly slaves; great incomes from corn and tobacco. They rode in chariots, with coachmen and footmen in livery. Their hunting-parties were led and followed by packs of dogs. Their Christmases were bountiful festivities, and their parties were brilliant with jewels, velvets, and brocades, powdered wigs, knee-breeches, ruffs, and trails.

The houses which still stand were not seemingly temporary structures, like many of the present day. They commanded grand views. They were solid with great porticos, like the home of Washington at Mount Vernon and the Lee house at Arlington.

The land was at peace, and yet the demands of the foreign government had begun to be deemed oppressive and this feeling was growing. The taxation of the people without representation in the House of Parliament was discussed as an injustice, and there was a growing feeling that the colonies ought to unite and have an independent government.

In Boston an organization called the Sons of Liberty was filling the air with the spirit of independence. The British authorities there found it difficult to maintain the peace against the rising spirit of revolution. The year 1775 found the New England colonies practically in arms against the taxation levied by the home government. Blood had been spilt at Concord and Lexington.

There was a song which the British soldiers in Boston had learned to sing in derision of the patriots. It had had its origin during the French war of 1755, twenty years before. The story of the song is as follows:

"During the attacks upon the French outposts in 1755, in America, Governor Shirley and General

Jackson led the force directed against the enemy lying at Niagara and Frontenac. In the early part of June, while these troops were stationed on the banks of the Hudson, near Albany, the descendants of the 'Pilgrim fathers' flocked in from the Eastern provinces. Never was seen such a motley regiment as took up its position on the left wing of the British army. The band played music as antiquated and *outré* as their *uniforms;* officers and privates had adopted regimentals each man after his own fashion; one wore a flowing wig, while his neighbor rejoiced in hair cropped closely to the head; this one had a coat with wonderful long skirts, his fellow marched without his upper garment; various as the colors of the rainbow were the clothes worn by the gallant band. It so happened that there was a certain Dr. Shackburg, wit, musician, and surgeon, and one evening after mess he produced a tune, which he earnestly commended, as a well-known piece of military music, to the officers of the militia. The joke succeeded, and Yankee Doodle became their march."

When Lord Percy was sent from Boston to reinforce the British troops at Lexington, an odd event happened in association with this song. Lord Percy's company marched to the tune of Yankee Doodle and went singing the song.

As the company marched out through Roxbury, a boy followed it laughing immoderately.

"And what are you laughing at, my lad?" asked Lord Percy.

"I am thinking how you will look when you return, dancing to the tune of Chevy Chase."

The tune was associated with the old Scottish ballad of that name. Lord Percy's great ancestor had fallen at the battle of Chevy Chase, and the boy's words haunted him and caused him to be depressed in spirits.

An encounter between the British soldiers and a mob, called the "Boston Massacre," which had been brought about by a negro by the name of Crispus Attucks in the year 1770, on the 5th of March, was celebrated by patriotic orations in the Old South Church as the date fell on each year. These yearly meetings became more and more a bolder war-cry for liberty. The government in 1775 had wished to prevent a renewal of the gathering of the patriots on the 5th of March.

Late in February of that year, Washington had summoned Harry Mendell to Williamsburg.

"I am advised by the burgesses," he said, "to send a courier to Boston on a secret mission to Samuel Adams. I have chosen *you*."

Harry's heart swelled with emotion. He was a young man now.

"I am at your service," said he.

"Then here are the letters. Go at once, and study the sentiments of the people while you are there."

Harry swiftly crossed the country by the way of Baltimore, Philadelphia, and Springfield. He arrived in Boston on March 6th. As the 5th had this year fallen on Sunday, the yearly patriotic meeting in the Old South Church was to take place on the 6th, on the morning of which he delivered the messages to Samuel Adams.

It was a day of strange events, and we give them as they used to be related in the old Boston families, which local history has, as we think, never been disproved.

The 6th of March, 1776, broke gray and cool on the windy wharves of Boston. The people were early in the streets despite the north wind. That day Joseph Warren, the patriot, was to deliver an oration on the Boston massacre in the Old South Church. He was a young man, and he loved the liberties of the people more than his own life, and his heart was no longer his own, but of his cause. The Sons of Liberty were to be present on that occasion, and the British officers. The early light of the morning found the patriots' flag flying from the Liberty Tree. One may see its effigy in stone now on Washington Street, near Boylston Street, on the building that stands where the grand old tree stood.

The town was full of excitement that morning. Men breathed fast and hurried. Their faces were electric. They stopped now and then to exchange views. Then hurried again. They hardly knew why they hurried. Something was in the air. The thrilling question in all minds was: "Would the British officers arrest Warren, Adams, Hancock, and the patriots that day in the Old South Church? Would it be a day of crisis, a day of fate?"

The Province House Indian vane turned to and fro in the March winds like the shifts of public opinion. Men's thoughts that day were as shifting as the air. At ten o'clock the whole town seemed to be in the streets. The Old South Church, near the windy harbor, began to fill with people. Hundreds of visitors from the neighboring towns had come riding into the town, some in wagons and some on horseback, and knots of excited men were to be seen about the stores and under the waving limbs of the bare trees on the Common.

British officers, in red coats and bright buttons, moved about in a body among the people, in a pompous, official, vice-regal way. One of these was observed to have in his hand an egg, and to show it to the others and to talk in a confidential way.

A bright boy, whom we will call Rodney, came tripping down a side street to the place were these officers were gathered and stopped and glanced curiously at the egg.

"Boy," said the stately looking soldier who held the egg, "you are a loyalist?"

"Yes, captain."

"And you are true to the cause of the king?"

"Yes, captain, that I am, sir."

"Your father is a loyalist?"

"Yes, captain."

"Do you know General Warren when you see him?"

"Yes, captain."

"Are you going to the South Church?"

"Yes—I will follow you there, sir."

"Boy, mark ye. That egg stands for King George. Don't you break it. In Queen Charlotte's name, don't break it. Throw it at him in the middle of his speech. Understand? Great events will follow."

"At Warren?"

"Yes, at Warren—Joseph Warren. Who did you think I said?"

The officer handed the egg to the boy, as though it were a sword and commission. As Rodney took it another officer remarked:

"If you fail, it may lose the king his colony."

The officers started for the church. They were a brilliant-looking company of men. Rodney, the boy, followed them.

The church was full of people. The British officers could hardly make their way to the seats in front of the platform which had been reserved for them, so dense was the excited crowd.

The boy concealed the egg in his hand and sleeve and stood alone in full view of the platform, just inside the door. The officer who had given him the egg sat down on the pulpit stairs under the black desk in view of the boy. Each glanced after the other.

Rodney began to think for the first time of the real importance of the position in which he was placed. He well understood that the throwing of the egg was to be the signal for the arrest of Warren, Adams, Hancock, and the leading patriots. The destiny of an empire might be in his hands. And Queen Charlotte—if he failed, what would Queen Charlotte say?

The people continued to gather and to crowd upon one another. And, hark! Outside a chorus of song burst upon the air. The words and music are thrilling:

> "Not the glitter of arms, nor the dread of a fray,
> Can make us submit unto chains for a day."

The chorus swelled:

> " For Freedom we're born,
> And, like sons of the brave,
> We'll never surrender,
> But swear to defend her,
> And scorn to survive if unable to save."

Rodney began to breathe the atmosphere of excitement and to have a sense of awe and fear. What would be the consequence to *him* should he throw the egg at Joseph Warren? He thought of Queen Charlotte.

The song rang on:

> " Then join hand in hand, brave Americans all,
> To be free is to live, to be slaves is to fall.
> Has the land such a dastard as scorns not a lord,
> Who dreads not the fetter far more than the sword?
>   For Freedom we're born,
>   And, like sons of the brave,
>   We'll never surrender,
>   But swear to defend her,
> And scorn to survive if unable to save."

The excitement grew. The people pressed one upon another. Eleven o'clock came. The orator had not arrived.

" He has been arrested," said one.

It was a false report, but it flew. There was a look

15

in the faces of the patriots that was anxious and awful. It seemed like the shadow of an oncoming tempest. One could feel in the palpitating air its influence, its import and meaning. The boy began to gaze about wildly and to tremble, but he carefully guarded the egg. He held it tight. He thought of Queen Charlotte, and squeezed it as firmly as King George squeezed the revenues of the empire. The pulpit was draped in black. It looked ominous and foreboding. Samuel Adams was there in his seat, John Hancock in his seat, the Sons of Liberty in their places. Women were there with stately bonnets, gray gowns, and white, anxious faces. The doors and aisles were full of firm-set lips and glancing eyes.

The slow minutes passed, but Warren did not come. There was a deep silence that became oppressive. It was thirty minutes past the hour. Had he been arrested?

Then there was a clatter at the great window of the church. A figure rose up before that gray light in full view of the startled congregation, like a spectre. It was the form of Warren in the dark robes of an orator.

The window was lifted. Hearts beat faster, and all eyes were fixed upon the beautiful face and the dark robes of the young patriot. Warren had been

unable to make his way through the crowd, and he
had gone up to the side of the church and mounted
a ladder, and so entered by the great pulpit window,
whose historic panes had rattled in the winds that
shattered the fleet of D'Auville that had been sent
out for the destruction of Boston.

The scene awed all. Every eye and ear were
strained. Every form sought to bend forward and
listen. Slowly, solemnly, came the first words of the
orator:

"It is not without the most humiliating conviction
of my want of ability that I now appear before you."

The people pressed upon each other in their eager-
ness to hear.

"I mourn over my bleeding country."

Eyes moistened and the air became electric with
sympathy. The orator's words flamed. His face
glowed. He burst into a strain of passionate elo-
quence and described the scene of the massacre on
the 5th of March:

"The baleful images of terror crowd around me,
and discontented ghosts, with hollow groans.

"Approach we the melancholy walk of death—

"We wildly stare about, and with amazement ask,
Who spread this ruin around us? Has haughty
France or cruel Spain sent forth her myrmidons?
Has the grim savage rushed again from the far wilder-

ness? No, none of these. It is the hand of Britain that inflicts the wound!"

At this point of profound sensitiveness, the officer thought that his opportunity had come. He glanced at the boy and the lad raised his trembling arm and his face turned white. Rodney felt something cutting his hand. He relinquished his grasp a little and gasped.

The egg was broken. What would Queen Charlotte say now? He opened his hand wider. There, broken beyond hope, was the egg of King George's empire. The yolk was flowing.

The officer looked at him sternly.

"Rodney," he said.

The boy tried to release his arm from the crowd around him, when he felt another crack in the frail egg, caused by an involuntary contraction of his hand. Just then a thrilling episode arrested all eyes.

A British officer, sitting on the pulpit stairs under Warren, held up his hand; in the fingers were three bullets.

Warren saw it. He read the menace in the movement. He held in his hand a white handkerchief. With a graceful and gracious movement of his hand the orator dropped the white handkerchief over the bullets in the hand of the officer. The scene thus represented to the fancy a menace of war and a proffer of peace, and so it was interpreted by all eyes.

The officer looked at the boy again and saw that he was crying.

"Where justice is the standard," continued the orator, "Heaven is the warrior's shield; but conscious guilt unnerves the arm that lifts the sword against the innocent."

The eloquent appeal continued:

"Having redeemed your country and secured the blessing to future generations, you cry, the glorious work is done. Then drop the mantle on some young Elisha and take your seats with kindred spirits in your native skies."

The boy worked his way through the crowd and fled from the church, leaving the egg behind. He thought of Queen Charlotte and felt like one who had somehow unhinged the order of the world.

Such was the day that Harry first spent in Boston.

There was one thought that had ridden with Harry all the way. It was that he might find the "courier from Boston," whom his mother had met on the Potomac. But the days of Governor Shirley were over. Who the courier was no one knew, not even the old council which had met at the Province House in Governor Shirley's days.

He consulted the patriots Samuel and John Adams

and General Warren about the matter.   They treated him with consideration, but were unable to offer any information or suggestion.   Governor Shirley had evidently acted very privately in the matter and sent some one in his personal service.

He returned to Virginia on March 23d, while the Convention of Delegates was in session, and returned to Washington letters from Samuel Adams and brought to other leading Virginians letters from John Adams and General Warren.

His ears were still ringing with Warren's address.

The Convention of Delegates on that day were enacting a scene similar to that he had witnessed in the Old South Church in Boston, though not in the presence of an armed enemy.

There was a lawyer in Virginia at this time who had been regarded by some people as especially stupid.   His name was Patrick Henry.   He was to speak that day on the subject of resistance to the British government, and the people who were assembled wondered as to how he would treat the momentous issue.

The house was crowded, and Harry could but recall the recent scene in the Old South.

The young orator rose.   He was not handsome in figure.   He was awkward, and his beginning was unpromising and slow.   But presently sentence after

sentence rolled from his lips which riveted all eyes
upon him and caused the assembly to be silent as
death. His words had a terrible earnestness, and his
manner grew more and more impressive. He did not
shriek as modern school-boys have done in repeating
the fateful address of that day, nor even seek declam-
atory force. His words were spoken in a deep, low
tone that made the heart beat slow. The earnestness of his solemn and subdued voice carried every
thought to the strained ears with convincing power.
He said:

"This, sir, is no time for ceremony. The question
before the house is one of awful moment to this
country. For my own part, I consider it as nothing
less than a question of freedom or slavery; and in
proportion to the magnitude of the subject ought to
be the freedom of the debate. It is only in this way
that we can hope to arrive at truth and fulfil the
great responsibility which we hold to God and our
country. Should I keep back my opinions at this
time through fear of giving offence, I should consider
myself as guilty of treason toward my country and of
an act of disloyalty toward the majesty of Heaven,
which I revere above all earthly kings.

"Mr. President, it is natural to man to indulge in
the illusions of hope. We are apt to shut our eyes
against a painful truth and listen to the song of that

siren till she transforms us into beasts. Is this the part of wise men engaged in a great and arduous struggle for liberty? Are we disposed to be of the number of those who, having eyes, see not, and having ears, hear not, the things which so nearly concern their temporal salvation? For my part, whatever anguish of spirit it may cost, I am willing to know the whole truth, to know the worst and to provide for it.

"I have but one lamp by which my feet are guided, and that is the lamp of experience. I know of no way of judging of the future but by the past. And judging by the past, I wish to know what there has been in the conduct of the British ministry for the last ten years to justify those hopes with which gentlemen have been pleased to solace themselves and the house? Is it that insidious smile with which our petition has been lately received? Trust it not, sir; it will prove a snare to your feet. Suffer not yourselves to be betrayed with a kiss. Ask yourselves how this gracious reception of our petition comports with those warlike preparations which cover our waters and darken our land.

"Are fleets and armies necessary to a work of love and reconciliation? Have we shown ourselves so unwilling to be reconciled that force must be called in to win back our love? Let us not deceive ourselves, sir. These are the implements of war and subjugation, the last arguments to which kings resort. I ask, sir, what means this martial array, if its purpose be not to force us to submission? Can gentlemen assign any other possible motive for it? Has Great Britain any enemy in this quarter of the world, to call for all this accumulation of navies and armies? No, sir, she has none. They are meant for us; they can be meant for no other. They are sent over to bind and rivet upon us those chains which the British ministry have been so long forging. And what have we to oppose them? Shall we try argument? Sir, we have been trying that for the last ten years. Have we anything new to offer upon the subject? Nothing. We have held the subject up in every light of which it is capable, but it has been in vain. Shall we resort to entreaty and humble supplication? What terms shall we find which have not been already exhausted? Let us not, I beseech you, sir, deceive ourselves longer.

"Sir, we have done everything that could be done to avert the storm that is now coming on. We have petitioned, we have remonstrated, we have supplicated, we have prostrated ourselves before the throne and have implored its interposition to arrest the tyrannical hands of the ministry and Parliament. Our petitions have been slighted; our remonstrances have produced additional violence and insult; our supplications have been disregarded, and we have been spurned with contempt from the foot of the throne.

"In vain, after these things, may we indulge the fond hope of peace and reconciliation. There is no longer any room for hope. If we wish to be free, if we mean to preserve inviolate those inestimable privileges for which we have been so long contending, if we mean not basely to abandon the noble struggle in which we have been so long engaged, and which we have pledged ourselves never to abandon until the glorious object of our contest shall be obtained, we must fight! I repeat it, sir, we must fight! An appeal to arms and to the God of hosts is all that is left us!

"They tell us, sir, that we are weak—unable to cope with so formidable an adversary. But when shall we be stronger? Will it be the next week or the next year? Will it be when we are totally disarmed and when a British guard shall be stationed in every house? Shall we gather strength by irresolution and inaction? Shall we acquire the means of effectual resistance by lying supinely on our backs and hugging the delusive phantom of hope until our enemies shall have bound us hand and foot? Sir, we are not weak if we make a proper use of those means which the God of nature hath placed in our power.

".Three millions of people armed in the holy cause of liberty, and in such a country as that which we possess, are invincible by any force which our enemy can send against us. Besides, sir, we shall not fight our battles alone. There is a just God who presides over the destinies of nations and who will raise up friends to fight our battles for us.

"The battle, sir, is not to the strong alone; it is to the vigilant, the active, the brave. Besides, sir, we have no election. If we were base enough to desire it, it is now too late to retire from the contest. There is no retreat but in submission and slavery! Our chains are forged. Their clanking may be heard on the plains of Boston! The war is inevitable, and let it come! I repeat it, sir, let it come!

"It is vain, sir, to extenuate the matter. Gentlemen may cry peace, peace, but there is no peace. The war has actually begun! The next gale that sweeps from the north will bring to our ears the clash of resounding arms! Our brethren are already in the field! Why stand we here idle? What is it that gentlemen wish? What would they have? Is life so dear or peace so sweet as to be purchased at the price of chains and slavery? Forbid it, Almighty God! I know not what course others may

take, but as for me, give me liberty or give me
death!"

Harry had heard Joseph Warren and Patrick
Henry speak on the same subject, and he knew that
a crisis was at hand. He recalled his mother's words,
and in the events to come, be they what they would,
he was resolved to be "true to the best that was in
him."

He became a trusted courier during the Revolution.

His last commission was both joyful and sad. It
was to bear to Mary Washington the news that York-
town had surrendered, and messages to Winchester where Lord Fairfax now was.

The streets of Winchester rang with cheers when
Harry proclaimed the great news in the town. Lord
Fairfax was making a visit there at the time. He
heard the cheering in the streets.

The Baron of Cameron was more than ninety years
of age now and still a royalist. Harry found him
in his arm-chair, white-haired and thin.

"My lord, I am the bearer of great news—Cornwallis has surrendered."

He looked up as one disappointed, and all the blood
left his face.

"Surrendered—to George?"

"Yes—to Washington."

Greenway Court.

"It is time for me to die. Joe, take me to my bed and turn my face to the wall."

The old black servant took the baron to his bed, as though he were a baby, and laid him down. He never rose again.

An old ballad tells the story in the spirit of the minstrel's art:

"Then uprose Joe all at the word
  And took his master's arm,
And to his bed he softly led
  The lord of Greenway Farm.
And thrice he called on Britain's name,
  And thrice he wept full sore,
Then sighed, O Lord, thy will be done!
  And word spake never more."

They bore the body of the lonely old man to his last resting-place among the lovely hills of the Shenandoah. The Episcopal church of Winchester now stands over his grave and holds his memorial tablet and his coat-of-arms.

The leaves in the forest were falling as they bore his body to rest. It was a sad day for the people he had known. All felt that a great soul had gone out of the Shenandoah.

After the last rites Harry went to Greenway Court.

He looked back into the deserted rooms. The great trees around the door were bare; the merry swifts were gone; the old dogs howled in the kennels. He thought of the ivied castles of which he had heard the old lord speak; of the faded events of English history through which the blood of the Fairfaxes had flowed; of the gay scenes of the lord's early days as he had heard them pictured; of Washington's young life here; of young Shirley; of the glittering troopers that came with Braddock; of the dark tragedies of the French and Indian war.

It was ended now; the light of the old days were faded and gone. The old lord had never been able to see her destiny. He had been an actor in the grand events that made America free, but had never intended to render to liberty such a service. He had builded better than he knew, and love, honor, and pity have kept the mosses from ever gathering about his grave, but set the church of the cross above him, and the world will ever remember him as a grand and noble influence in the young life of Washington.

CHAPTER XX.

AFTER MANY DAYS—A JOURNEY TO PHILADELPHIA— HARRY MENDELL AND THE PRESIDENT.

IN the valley where a large part of the city of Washington now stands was once a plantation. The cottage was humble and may still be seen in the yard of the old Van Ness mansion, near the Washington Monument. The owner of this plantation was a rough, plain-spoken man, a merry old Scotchman, named David Burns.

Of all the plantations on the Potomac, this was perhaps the most beautiful in situation. It was surrounded by a circle of hills among which the Potomac flowed. The river had large and fertile marshes, the uplands were rich in soil, and the surrounding forests were old and noble.

Washington had seen this beautiful valley when a young surveyor. He seems always to have dreamed of it; for when he was commissioned by Congress to select a spot for a national capital, his mind at once turned to this hill-circled valley through which the Potomac flowed.

He attempted to purchase the plantation for national use, but old David Burns, or Davie Burns, as he was called, was obstinate and refused to sell it. At last Washington, having the authority to use any part of the national domain for the site of the capital, went to the Scotchman to tell him that he had decided to occupy this valley for the purpose, and that liberal compensation would be made to him for his lands.

"You think," said the old Scotchman, "that everything is grain for your hopper. Who would you have been had you not married the widow Custis?"

We quote Davie's own words nearly as spoken; for the answer is a part of local history. On Davie Burns' plantation the city of Washington was founded. Here the old Scotchman, however, continued to live, and here grew up his beautiful daughter Marcia Burns, who married a wealthy Congressman by the name of Van Ness. It was at the cottage of David Burns that Tom Moore was entertained while in Washington. Mr. Van Ness erected the grand mansion whose ruined porticoes and gardens may still be visited, and which became famous for its hospitalities in the early days of the city. The Presidents and Congressmen of those early days used to be enter-

tained here, and there is a poetic legend that the
white horses on the place all died of grief when Mr.
Van Ness himself passed away, and that they still appear at midnight on Christmas Eve in the beautiful
grounds.

Marcia Burns Van Ness founded the Washington
Orphan Asylum, and her beautiful portrait may still
be seen there. When she died the Government
stopped business for a day. Her tomb, a temple of
Vesta in the Georgetown cemetery near the city, is
often visited. It is near the spot where sleeps the
author of " Home, Sweet Home." She lived much in
her father's old cottage, close to her grand mansion,
in her last years. The cottage is now a part of the
old Van Ness gardens.

Harry Mendell, after his life as a war courier and
bearer of dispatches was ended, entered the service of
David Burns as a manager of his great estate.

He liked the honest old Scotchman, and he learned
to know the Potomac country well and how to culti-
vate the fertile farms. The elevation where the Capitol now stands had a peculiar charm for him, as he
had heard that Washington had said that here was
the place for a city.

One summer day, when the forest was full of wild
roses and the songs of birds, Harry was resting his
team on the side of the hill where the Capitol gar-

dens now spread their green hedges around the work of art. He saw a boat coming up the river. Few boats were seen on the river then, and he left his team and went down to the marshes to meet it. A negro was in it.

"Is this Massa Burns' place?" asked the negro as he saw Harry.

"Yes.   What is wanted?"

"Do you live here?"

"Yes."

"Do you know, please sar, do you know a person named Harry Mendell?"

"I am the man."

"Then you be de berry man I's sent to see.   Do you know Mr. Rouzé?"

"I ought to.   He brought me up.   I would do anything for him."

"You would, hey?"

"Yes."

"You'll hab a chance, then.   Do you want ter know where he is?"

"Yes—where?"

"In jail."

"*In jail!*"

"Yes, and he has sent you dis."

The negro boatman handed Harry a letter.

He tore it open and read:

"WILLIAMSBURG, VA.

"DEAR HARRY:

"I am in distress, in jail. I stood by you like a father when you were in distress. I need *you* now; I hope you will stand by me as a son. I once prevented you from going to jail, and now I want you to get me out of jail. I know your heart, Harry Mendell. It is gold.

"How did I come to be in jail? Loveland. He has been made an agent of Washington's estates and business affairs, with authority to collect debts.

"You remember that two hundred pounds that I borrowed of Washington when you lived with me. I have never been able to pay it. It became due long ago. I struggled to raise the money, but my large family must have bread, and so it was impossible. Heaven knows how hard I have worked and how many worried nights I have passed. The debt has haunted me for years.

"When Washington's affairs came into Loveland's hands he sued me. He would have taken my lands, but land cannot be taken for debt except by the owner's consent. I know that Washington would not like to have my land taken for the debt. I refused to sign away the land until I consulted with my friends.

"You are my friend. So is Washington. If Washington demands it he can have my land, and I can become a laborer for others or I can slave. But, Harry Mendell, George Washington will never demand of me my house. He will release me at once. I know him as I know you.

"Will you ride to Philadelphia for me, and see President Washington and tell him that Reuben Rouzé is in jail for debt?

"If you will, you will repay me for all the unselfish love I once gave you. You see the whole case and my situation. I can trust you and Washington. Oh, what different fates we have all had—the boys of Greenway Court!

        " With a father's love,

                        " REUBEN ROUZÉ."

Harry dropped the letter by his side.

" Can you see Mr. Rouzé?" he asked of the boatman.

" Yes, sar."

" How?"

" It was the sheriff sent me, sar."

" I see. Tell him—listen now—tell him that I will go. Tell him that I will make the swiftest ride that ever was made from Alexandria to Philadelphia, and that I will return with Washington's message to Williamsburg. Do you understand?"

" I understand."

The boatman rowed away on the calm summer river. Harry hurried to his team. In an hour he had told the story to old David Burns, and soon was flying on the Scotchman's swiftest horse over the Maryland hills.

Harry rode to Philadelphia over the old post route, and the way was direct and not long. He entered the city in the early morning. He drew his rein before the old State-house, and thought of the Liberty bell and its wonderful history.

Another scene rose before him. It was of the Oc-

tober morning when he rode toward Fredericksburg
and Greenway Court, to convey the news of the
surrender of Lord Cornwallis. Lieutenant-Colonel
Tilghman, an aide of Washington, had been dispatched to Philadelphia to announce the same news to
Congress, then in session.

This officer came to the city at night. A watch-
man was passing to and fro, swinging his lantern
and crying:

"Past twelve o'clock, and all is well!"

The lieutenant knocked at the door of the house
of the President of the Congress. The knock failed
to arouse the house. He pounded. The watchmen,
supposing him to be some seditious or disorderly
person, were about to cause his arrest, when he announced the news that decided the fate of America
and was to startle the world.

The watchmen went on their way joyfully, crying:

"Past one o'clock, and Cornwallis has surrendered!"

Lights began to flash in the windows, shutters to
bang, and doors to open. Men ran shouting through
the streets:

"Cornwallis has surrendered!"

The bells rang. The whole city awoke. There
was a morning illumination of the houses. Presently
the old Liberty bell, that had rung joy and storm on

the day of the adoption of the Declaration, added its melodious tones to the clanging jubilee.

"Past three o'clock, and Cornwallis is taken! A cold and frosty morning!"

The members of the Continental Congress were in the streets. They met here and there in large groups, and decided that the first thing to be done was to pass a resolution to go to one of the churches and give thanks to God.

"Past four o'clock!"

"Past five o'clock!"

It was morning now. The light was lifting over the Schuylkill and the first day of Independence dawned upon the joyful city—the first day at least that the people's Congress knew that the nation was free.

Harry first went to the old slate-roofed house that had been occupied by William Penn and that had been the state residence of John Adams. Here he passed the night, and early in the morning rode to Germantown.

He there met President Washington.

"You are welcome, my old friend," said the President. "But some urgency has brought you here at this early hour. I hope that you bring good news, as you used to carry good news during the war."

"I came to bring you bad news, but I hope that you will make me the bearer of good news, as at York-town. My errand is a very simple one."

"Deliver it—I hope I may be of service to you."

"My friend, Reuben Rouzé, is in trouble."

"I am sorry to hear it. He is a generous, well-meaning man. I have befriended him and I would be glad to do so again. He is a true man in the day of trouble."

"It is in your power to again befriend him. He has been arrested for debt."

"Arrested! by whom?"

"Loveland, in your name!"

"Arrested in my name! I never intended that that note should be presented to him for collection by any one but myself. Where is Mr. Rouzé now?"

"In jail!"

"In jail?"

"Yes, he sent for me to bear you this letter."

Washington read the letter. He was angry. He felt that injustice had been done not only to his old neighbor, but to himself.

He sat for a time in thoughtful silence, then taking a pen, said:

"I will order his release immediately. Mr. Rouzé has been a true neighbor to me. I will cancel the debt wholly. Kindly return to him and convey to

him my expressed confidence and esteem, and oblige
me by handing this letter to Loveland. A more
severe reprimand will follow."

The President spoke of Greenway Court and the
hospitable days of the old lord, and of the boys who
were now statesmen or who had died in their
country's service.

"The old lord little thought that when he was so
eager to see the colonies united against the French,
the movement was one tending to independence of
the Crown," said Harry.

"Have you been to the Court since he died?"

"Yes, your honor, once."

"What did you see there?"

"I recall but two things, an empty chair and the
golden horseshoe hanging over the fireplace. President Washington, I can never forget the strange
event that brought me there. You can never tell
what I have suffered from my honor being called
into question by those circumstances. Did you ever
hear who Governor Shirley's courier from Boston
was?"

"No; but why trouble yourself in regard to that
matter? There is no one who to-day believes that
you were intentionally dishonest or untruthful or
that you were in any way to blame. You have lived
down all suspicions."

"But, President Washington, I wish to *prove* my honor. You would: any man stituated as I am would. I feel sure—it haunts me like a conviction—that Governor Shirley's courier could tell me something that would make my story clear."

"Governor Shirley's family might give you some information in regard to the courier. They still live in Roxbury."

"My poor old mother used to say, 'Be true to the best that is in you.' I owe it to my friends as well as myself to try to make my honor clear. As soon as Reuben Rouzé is released I shall ride to Boston again, my own courier in the cause of my own honor."

CHAPTER XXI.

REUBEN ROUZÉ IS RELEASED.

ARRY MENDELL delivered Washington's letter to Mr. Loveland, who read it with surprise and saw that the spirit which he had shown in the matter had made him a discredited man in the President's view and that the loss of his character would follow.

Reuben Rouzé was released.

Harry rode home with his old friend from the jail.

The meeting of Mr. Rouzé with his wife and children was most tender and affecting.

"I owe it all to Harry," said Mr. Rouzé. "Did ever a man have a better friend?"

"Yes, I," said Harry. "What could I have been had it not been for you?"

"Every event in life has soul," said Mr. Rouzé, "and that soul lives. My thoughts for others in the past come back to me to-day."

He sat down among his family with tears in his eyes.

238

"Wife, George Washington has discharged the debt, but that does not release me from my duty to pay it."

"As a matter of honor and gratitude, we should pay it," said Mrs. Rouzé, "even if we have to live poorly."

"Yes, I am willing to live poorly—to suffer to save money to pay that debt. It would be a proud day for us to put that money into Washington's hands. Our children would remember it. It would make my heart light and free again, and that would be happiness. We must do it."

"I will help you to do it," said Mrs. Rouzé.

The two sat for a time in silence, and the family of children gathered around their father and felt the seriousness of the scene.

Mrs. Rouzé was a religious woman. She at last broke the silence.

"I have a plan to remind us daily of our resolution. I shall instruct the children to pray daily for the health, prosperity, and protection of George Washington."

"And I will work to pay this debt of honor as though Washington had never caused it to be discharged."

The scene that we have described is nearly true to life, for the story of Reuben Rouzé's debt is true, and it is but an example of the old Virginian sense of honor.

"Mr. Rouzé," said Harry, "you have made a resolution to make your honor clear?"

"Yes, Harry."

"I have also."

"Your honor is clear now."

"The event of *that* night, my story, and poor mother's?"

"No one suspects you of any dishonor now."

"Loveland."

"Not even he, in his heart."

"He would be glad to do so. Any enemy that I may have would. No one must have the opportunity. Mr. Rouzé, I am going to Boston again!"

"Why?"

"To try to find the courier."

"Governor Shirley's old courier?"

"Yes: he who met my mother."

"Governor Shirley is dead."

"But his family are living."

"In Boston?"

"Yes."

"How do you know?"

"Washington has told me so."

"But they might not know who the courier was."

"But they might. I would feel that I had done my duty to my mother and to myself to see them."

"Can you afford to make the long journey, Harry?"

"Any one can afford to vindicate his honor."

Harry rose and stood for a moment in silence, and then said, quoting from an old poem:

> "My life and honor both together run;
> Take honor from me, and my life is done."

"Harry," said Mr. Rouzé, "you are a noble boy. The others have gained position and wealth, and they are worthy all, but there was no boy among the young men who were called the 'boys of Greenway Court' who was more worthy of respect than you; and he who gains his reward and he who merits but does not gain the same reward are equal in the eye of Heaven."

"I have ridden to Philadelphia for you. I shall now ride to Boston for myself. I will vindicate my word. Something within tells me so; something without tells me so. You will pay the debt. We may not have wealth or fame, but, Mr. Rouzé, we will have honor."

"When will you go, Harry?"

"To-morrow, while I have health, strength, and opportunity. I feel as though an invisible hand was pushing me to do this thing."

"You are an honorable courier, Harry. You should be awarded a golden horseshoe."

The dream of the faded days of Greenway Court rose before them, and amid those scenes the golden horseshoe shone again in their minds' eyes like a star.

CHAPTER XXII.

THERE stands in the Roxbury District of Boston the ruin of a stately colonial mansion that but few Bostonians themselves have seen. It is near the busy thoroughfare named Dudley Street, and only a few blocks back of the Dudley Street horse-car stables and the Hugh O'Brien Grammar School. It is the old Shirley House, on Shirley Street, or, as it was known in the early part of the present century, the Eustis House.

Its great, wide porticoes are gone; its grand halls have been cut up into cheap tenements, but its golden vane still turns in the shifting winds of the harbor, and its octagonal tower, diamond windows, and colonial doors recall the days when it was the queen of provincial mansions and the scene of vice-regal life. It was built by Governor Shirley, the heroic defender of the English cause against the French in America and one of the greatest of the ten colonial governors.

243

Here the beautiful Lady Shirley, whose tomb may be seen in King's Chapel, doubtless entertained English lords and the heroes of the French-English war. Here Washington, Franklin, Lafayette, Aaron Burr, and a host of early republican notables found a hospitable welcome. Here Governor Shirley's active life ended in 1771, leaving the mansion to his family.

The house stood on the side of a hill in Roxbury fields, overlooking Boston Harbor and Dorchester Bay. The views from its windows were most beautiful: the fields, the blue harbor, Point Shirley, and the ocean-ways. Boston lay, as it were, under it, and from the top of the hill the blue air of the hills of Milton delighted the eye.

Governor Shirley had a large family, but only one son survived him, who was knighted in England. His estate fell to his daughter Elizabeth, wife of Judge Hutchinson, and this family maintained its dignity until it became the property of Governor Eustis, and repeated in the early republic the social hospitalities of provincial days.

It is sad to see it now: its trees, orchards, and gardens gone, upstart houses and a foreign population crowding upon it, and divided into tenements for cheap rents. Boston should have kept sacred the Shirley House and Virginia Greenway Court.

It was to this house, in the days of its dignity, that

Harry Mendell came on one long June day, when the great orchards were going out of bloom and the gardens were filled with roses, and the blue harbors rippled calmly under the marsh meadow trees.

He was more than welcome to the Shirley-Hutchinson family. The fact that he had met and known young William Shirley and was with him when he fell at Braddock's defeat brought him at once into the most tender relations with the daughters of Governor Shirley, the sisters of the young hero. He was invited to spend the summer here, and every possible courtesy and kindness was extended to him. He withheld for a time the purpose of his visit.

One evening as the family were sitting on one of the two great porticoes that overlooked the sea, Harry said:

"I have not yet told you the real purpose of my visit. It is a matter that concerns my personal honor and also the word of my mother, long dead."

"You excite our curiosity," said Lady Shirley, one of the sisters.

"Your father had a courier?"

"Yes, several."

"He sent one of them to Williamsburg, Virginia, after he became a military man?"

"That is likely, my friend. He sent couriers to many places."

17

"Do you know who that courier was?"

"No—it must have been Major Henley. He was father's confidential courier. He was a relative of ours and very dear to us. He lived with us."

"May I ask where he is now?"

"He is dead."

"I am disappointed to hear you say that, Lady Shirley. I think that he once met my mother on the banks of the Potomac, in Virginia. She was an old woman then and was touched in mind. She claimed to have found a prize of great value to me and my honor when he was passing and to have shown it to him. It is that matter that I wish to verify."

"What was the prize, may I ask?"

"A horseshoe."

"One of Governor Spottswood's golden horse-shoes?"

"No, but one of more value to me than Governor Spottswood's own golden horseshoe, which was set with gems, I have been told."

"How so, my friend, if I may not be inquisitive?"

"From its associations. The finding of it concerns my personal honor, and if I only knew *where* it was found, the information might throw light on an event which is very mysterious to me and to others."

"Major Henley left his journals and private papers with us. I think that the family have never examined them. You are at liberty to consult them. Any extraordinary incident of an expedition might be found in his journal of that expedition. I do not know. Let us offer you the opportunity to investigate the matter."

The next day the journals and papers of Major William Henley, of the staff of ex-Governor Shirley, then a commandant, were laid before him. They constituted a manuscript library.

Harry examined them eagerly and carefully. He found that the journals were personal and very minute in detail.

He came to one at last that caused his heart to beat and his fingers to thrill. It was entitled "*A Journal of an Overland Journey to Williamsburg, Va., as a Courier to Governor Shirley.*"

He turned the leaves with a trembling hand. They were full of personal incidents.

He came to a certain page marked with red ink.

"*December 20th.*

"An odd incident occurred on the Potomac road.

"Met an old white-haired woman. Daft.

"She stood holding up a horseshoe which she had found driven into a spike on an old Virginia raft made of *sections of logs,* and which had some time washed ashore and been lodged among the bushes. She was shouting with delight and singing parts of hymns. I stopped and spoke to her, for I saw that she was out of her mind and I pitied her.

"She said that she had a son who had been accused of theft and lying, and that the finding of the horse-shoe would in some way vindicate his honor."

Harry glanced down the page. He started back, then bent forward again, and read slowly:

"I asked the old woman her son's name.

"She said it was HARRY MENDELL!"

Harry sat dumb. He saw it all now; how the horse had walked down the bank onto the raft; how that the weight of the horse had put the raft in motion; how that the rushing of the freshet water had carried it diagonally to the other shore, and how that he had *looked down between the sections* of the logs *into* the water when the moon for a moment had appeared.

"I feel to-day the same joy in my heart that was in her heart on that day," he said at last. "I have been true to the best that is in me. I HAVE PROVEN MY HONOR."

He showed the journal to young Lady Shirley and told her the story of his life.

"If I could own that journal," he said, "to show to my friends and to recall my struggles, it would make me happy."

"I assure you it will give us pleasure to give it to you," said Lady Shirley.

He left the Shirley House with the journal, a happy man. The country flew past him on his journey back.

And his happiness was renewed as he showed that journal to Reuben Rouzé and George Washington, and to the old people of the families of the Northern Neck who were once numbered among the boys of Greenway Court.

Harry Mendell's name was a crown of honor now wherever it was spoken. He needed no golden horseshoe to bear witness that he had been an honorable rider in the interest of every cause that was good and true.

He desired to go to Greenway Court once more and spend a day or two amid the associations of his young sad life. Why, he could not tell. It may have been because it was there he last saw his mother alive, and because he had loved the old Tory lord and had never forgotten the evening that the latter had told the story of his private life.

We have impressions that command us, and such an impression led him back to the low-roofed lodge on the slopes of the hills of the Shenandoah. He carried the journal with him.

The leaves were falling and the trees were bare. A relative of the old lord by the name of Martin now held the estate, and the scenes about the house

were changing as garments change with the wearers.
There was no baying of hounds, no gathering of
young negroes, no bustling, frowning, sneering
Loveland.   The place was still.

There was a small stone house near the Court that
Lord Fairfax had made his office.   Here he had
doubtless held interviews with young Washington
over maps and charts, and here Braddock may have
planned in visions and dreams a glorious and victo-
rious campaign.

The house has two windows and a door in front,
but is otherwise perfectly plain.   It was a place of
plans and dreams in the old lord's time, and many
schemes that influenced the destiny of the nation
doubtless had their origin here.

In this stone house, whose door stood open to the
sun, sat Nance, withered and gray, with a company
of negroes around her.

She started up as she saw Harry and cried: "Fo'
the Lor' sake!   All you-uns sit still now and saw
wood.   De conjured boy am come again, ridin' on de
horses of de air.

"Come in—come into de yard, Harry Mendell.
De ole lord he hab ascended up on high; and de
world am all turned upside down and down side up
and over and aroun'.   But it don't matter, for dese
am de las' times.   I was preachin' to my spiritual

chillen. Come in and hear what old Nance has to say, old Nance who walked by faith on de waters ob de Shenando'."

There was silence in the Court, for the owner had indeed gone away. Harry hitched his horse and approached the small stone house. The oak table and the chairs that the old lord had used were there, and the latter were filled by negroes, most of whom were young.

"I was a-preachin' to 'em for their final good," said old Nance, "for oh! the great thunder weather is coming, and some day it will be hard for dem wot have concealed the truth. My tex' is—Wot am my 'ead [head] fo'? wot am my 'ead fo'?

"Sit down, Massa Harry. The Lord has a message for you."

Harry sat down. The old woman looked at him distrustfully, stood in silent prayer for a little time with lifted face, and then seemed resolved to do her duty, whatever the consequences might be.

"Chillen, listen now: What am my 'ead fo'? I know what my feet am for, but they are now almost at the end of de long journey. I know wot my hands are fo'; and some of you will know if you don't sot still and listen. But wot am my 'ead fo'?

"It am to be de chamber ob de Lord. De Lord he am in dar now, and, chillens, I nebber yet feared de face of clay; oie Nance nebber feared de face of clay, and I am gwine to declare unto you de whole counsel ob de Lord. Ole Nance knows—she walked on de Shenando.'

"Wot am my 'ead fo'? It was to see wisions and dream dreams. Wot am my eyes for? Dey am to see de works of de Lord. Wot am my tongue for? It am to speak de trut'.

"De Bible says dat he dat hab anything on his soul, let 'im get up on de house-top and tell it. Chillens, hab any ob ye got anything upon your souls?

"Wot am my 'ead fo'? Brudder Ben, has you got anything upon your soul? If so, get up on de house-top and holler. For de thunder weather am comin', and you be sure to be foun' out. Sister Liza, hab you got anything upon your soul? If so, get up on de house-top and holler, for de thunder weather am comin' and you're shore to be foun' out! And, O ye young people all—you, Chloe, you, Crane, you, Stanton—hab you got any sin hidden in your souls? If so, get up on de house and tell it. 'Cause de clouds of adversity am gatherin' on de mountains, and you will hear de thunder drums rollin' right soon, and you-uns will all get found out. And you, young Jasper, I know dat you am a sinner; I can see —wot my 'ead fo'? You fly right up to de top and 'fess, for the great *Ethiopian* am comin' after his own folks pretty soon, and you'll be shore to be all found out."

She paused and lifted her black, bony hand in the air.

"An' now I hab a message to deliber. Wot my 'ead fo'? I hab a message to deliber, and it have been laid on my soul for years. Old Nance nebber yet feared de face of clay. Wot my 'ead fo'?

"Harry Mendell, hab *you* got anything on *your* soul? De Lord hab sent you to me. I can see. Wot my 'ead fo'? Harry Mendell, ye must answer now, shore as yer bawn. Harry Mendell, de two eyes of de Hebbens are upon ye. Answer me—it am last time, and I'll do my duty by yer now if I drop right down here onto the floor. Harry Mendell, think ob de past now and answer up. Hab ye got any lie in de pocket of yer soul?"

She looked at him with her black eyes fixed.

"No, aunty; Harry Mendell has not got any lie in the pocket of his soul, and never had. The horse *that* night crossed the river on a raft made of logs in sections. I spoke the truth then, as I thought it to be. It has all been found out."

Old Nance stood dazed. She lowered her hand slowly.

"I always knowed dat you was an honest man,

Harry Mendell. I knew it all; I can see. Wot am my head for? You ought to get up on the house-top like de 'postle and *crow*. I knew dat you was honest all de time. I saw it in a wision. Wot my 'ead fo'?"

The old woman sat down. She and her conscience did not seem quite at ease with each other. But she had stood by her reputation as a prophetess.

"I will forgive you the past, Nance," said Harry, as he rose up to walk about the place. "But I fear it is you who needs most to get up to the top of the house."

"Me, Harry? me, Harry Mendell? Me wot walked on de waters ob de Shenando'? Wot am my head for?"

He rode away, and never met old Nance again. He hardly could tell why he came, but it pleased him to have told the simple old negro woman the truth.

He left Greenway Court in the sunset and crossed the glimmering stream of the Shenandoah. He turned on the rising ground and gazed on the two bell-towers and shelving roof, and his eye once more moistened as he thought of the old lord who had wintered his barren years there. He fancied that he could now see the purpose of that lonely life. And he rode on.

CHAPTER XXIII.

REUBEN ROUZÉ PAYS HIS DEBT.

WASHINGTON had looked forward from the Presidential chair to the time when he should return to Mount Vernon and live again among his old neighbors as the great happiness that would crown his life. To his old friend, General Knox, he wrote as follows on the day before leaving his high office: "To the weary traveller who sees a resting-place and is bending his body thereon, I now compare myself. Although the prospect of a retirement is most grateful to my soul, and I have not a wish to mix again in the great world or to partake in its politics, yet I am not without regret at parting with, perhaps never more to meet, the few intimates whom I love. Among these be assured you are one."

On leaving the Presidency he had wished to return to Mount Vernon in a quiet way, but this could not be. His journey was a long triumphal progress. Cannon boomed, bells rang, triumphal arches spanned the streets of towns and villages, children strewed the way with flowers. The sentiment long afterward so well spoken by Henry Lee was already in the air: "First in war, first in peace, first in the hearts of his countrymen." The whole nation delighted to look up to him as the "father of his country."

He had been long in retirement before the reorganization of the American army was assigned him by President Adams. He accepted the trust reluctantly, under a sense of duty.

He was at home now among the scenes of his boyhood. He could meet those boys of Greenway Court who were left; he could ride down the Northern Neck or to Winchester or Williamsburg as in the buoyant days before the French empire in America fell.

He made an early visit to Reuben Rouzé. The Rouzé family had expected it, and they awaited it with pride. By hard work, economy, and self-denial they had saved two hundred pounds, the equivalent of one thousand dollars.

The wife and children, as well as the father, had toiled steadily to earn and save this sum. The whole family had entered into the struggle with pride, and the children had been denied the usual pastimes of youth that their father might one day meet Washington with a sense of honor.

He came, riding as of old on a spirited horse and

unattended.   He dismounted, and was welcomed with an expression of gladness that can only arise from an inward sense of worth.

"May it please your honor," said Mr. Rouzé, "I can never repay the debt of gratitude I owe you, but I have long awaited your coming as the best day of my life.   I have earned the money, with the help of my family, and my conscience and my hands are free."

"What money, my friend?"

"The two hundred pounds that you loaned me."

"I discharged that debt long ago, friend."

"But my conscience did not.   I was still held in honor to pay the debt."

"Then I discharge it again."

"But more than to my honor I owe it to a sense of grateful feeling to pay you all.   I should do it for your sake, for my own sake, and for my family's sake. Wife, bring to me the one thousand dollars."

The careworn woman brought the money.   The children were poorly clad, but their faces shone with delight.

"Here is the money we have earned, and in gratitude my children have prayed for you daily since your order released me from prison.   We shall never cease to bless your name."

"But I cannot take it, Mr. Rouzé.   Your family

have helped earn it; your children need it. How many children have you, Mr. Rouzé?"

"Five."

"Five, and you have placed in my hands one thousand dollars—two hundred pounds, as we used to call the sum."

He counted it over.

"Now, my children, sit down. I am going to make you all a present out of respect to the character of your father. Let us divide the money here."

And George Washington gave the money to the children with a face that beamed with joy.

"And now, friend Rouzé, we will be loving neighbors, and may you and your family prosper. Your foster-boy Harry has proven his honor and is doing well. He rendered good service as a courier during the war. The people ought not to forget him. Our veterans will soon have to give place to younger men, and the world needs the service of such as he."

Washington rode away under the great shadows of the summer trees.*

---

* This chapter may seem like a dream of fiction. It is so in part, but every essential incident of it is true.

CHAPTER XXIV.

THE GOLDEN HORSESHOE.

THE honor of Harry Mendell in maintaining the spirit of truth in a case where his conviction of what was true seemed improbable, had left a definite impression in the minds of those statesmen who were once numbered among the boys of Greenway Court, but were now the leaders of thought in the young State of Virginia and in the new and growing republic. Right-doing has the gravitation that leads to public respect, as wrong-doing carries with it the law of its own disgrace and punishment. It is an impulse of the human heart, a natural and eternal principle, to reward and honor one who has spoken the truth to his own disadvantage.

Those who were left of the boys of Greenway Court, now turning gray, had never forgotten the poor boy's unwilling ride, his strange story, his unfortunate mother, and the remarkable ways in which his story had been proven to be true. His services in the Revolution as a courier had been noble. The other "boys of Greenway Court" had been rewarded for their patriotism by places of public trust. The honor of none in the maintenance of principle had been greater than that of Harry Mendell. How should his worth be recognized?

The militia of Virginia was to be reorganized now that the province had become a State. To this duty Harry was assigned, first with the rank of major, then of colonel, then of general. His conduct in this work was so wise, just, and unselfish as to commend him to the old Virginia officers. The veterans of the war, who might naturally be jealous of the sudden advancement of one who until late had been a non-commissioned officer, caught the popular sentiment and were glad to do honor to Harry Mendell.

That was a gala day in Virginia when the State militia met, after the proclamation of peace, to elect a commander-in-chief. The veterans of the war were there as special guests. Washington was to be present at the grand review; the Fairfaxes, the Lees, the old burgesses, and the young representatives of the provincial families of the Northern Neck. The governor was to be there and hold a reception in the evening. The legislature was in session and the members were invited to attend the reception.

Who should be elected the commander-in-chief of the new army of peace? The veteran officers were asked for advice in the matter and held a council. None of them desired the honor; like Washington himself, they wished for rest from the scenes and duties of military life.

"It should be a young man," said one of the old officers.

"And one who merits honor and has not received it," said another—"a young man of worth. The character of the people is known by the character of the men that the people honor."

"Harry Mendell," said a Revolutionary colonel. "He was a poor boy, but so was Franklin, and we are a republic now. It is character that makes men here, and in a republic character must be everything."

"Character is everything everywhere," said another veteran. "The name of Harry Mendell has come to stand for honor, justice, and worth. It would honor us to recommend him. I move that we so honor ourselves by giving him the nomination. How many approve of this as the sense of the council?"

Every officer responded "Ay."

Harry Mendell was elected that day with a loud acclamation. The old officers and soldiers of the Revolution uncovered their heads to him. Washington himself raised his hat to him as he came riding past him at the grand review. The children strewed

18

flowers before him as he marched at the head of the militia into camp.

That evening there was a reception given to the newly elected officers, in the old State-house of Williamsburg. Lady Washington, the pride of the Virginia families and the first lady in the country, was there. Burgesses were there in their old court costumes; officers in gold lace; women in brocades.

The next night a reception was held in the Apollo Room of the old Raleigh Tavern, in honor of the presence in town of General Daniel Morgan, the so-called "thunderbolt of the Revolution." The reception was to be conducted by Rose Page, of the family of an illustrious Virginia governor and statesman; a lady who represented the worthiest and most patriotic society and who was famous for her grace and beauty.

Washington was to be there; Madison, afterward President of the United States; old soldiers, military men, members of Congress, clergymen, and many representative men had been invited. The leading ladies of the society of the Virginia capital were to be there. The event was to be even more brilliant than that of the evening before.

Morgan had come to the Virginia capital from his farm near Winchester to meet the old officers of the war. His fidelity to truth during the campaigns caused him to be especially regarded at this time. When, after the battle of Saratoga, an attempt had been made to supersede General Washington by General Gates, Morgan had replied:

"Never mention that detestable subject to me again."

He was a sharer in the virtues of the wars, but had received only small rewards. This reflection caused him to be very popular among all classes of people— to be regarded as a Cincinnatus or a Regulus.

The Apollo Room at an early hour on that evening was resplendent with light. Chariots came to the door of the old Raleigh Tavern, left the guests in silks and brocades, and passed on. Men came in wigs, velvet coats, satin vests, and knee-buckles. There was a sound of violins, and at nine o'clock the music of the "Stately Minuet," as the Mozart or Don Giovanni minuet was called, again thrilled the pulses of the crowds in the waiting-rooms.

The crier took his place at the door, and Rose Page, surrounded by stately dames and jewelled maidens, formed a circle near him to receive the guests as they appeared.

"GENERAL GEORGE WASHINGTON AND LADY WASHINGTON," called the crier through the hall.

Grave and noble the first couple in the land moved slowly in to the gay, measured music.

The years of the active life of Washington were
over.   The mighty reality of the past lay behind him.
Yet it ever gave him delight to do honor to an old
soldier.

"JOHN MARSHALL!"

The once penniless soldier was tall, pale, and thin.
He wore a plain suit of black and was the picture of
republican simplicity.

The crowd filled the doors.   Lady Madison, followed
by a train of guests, was announced by the crier.
There was a long roll of the Lees and Ashes and
Henrys, and the crier seemed like a school-boy repeating a lesson in history.

"THE COURIERS OF THE WAR!"

The band that had introduced the scene by the
"Stately Minuet" now played "See, the Conquering
Hero Comes," as Daniel Morgan, one of the couriers,
was the name of honor to-night.

There was a hush in the gay assembly.   The guests
opened a way for the two couriers.   The first courier
was Daniel Morgan and the other was Harry Mendell.
They passed into the hall arm in arm, and the band
returned to the "Stately Minuet" again, and the company saluted each other with the first low bows of
the courtly ceremony.

Daniel Morgan and Harry Mendell were unused to
scenes like these.   They stood alone together in the

Presenting the golden horseshoe.

maze of poetic motion, and each thought of the past. Harry thought of the lonely grave of his mother, of all she had suffered and taught him.

"Old Morgan," as he was called, wore the sword that the nation had given him, and a gold medal of honor shone on his breast. He glanced at the golden stars that the old veterans wore and said:

"I care little, Harry, for all of this pomp and gayety. My conscience has conquered me, and I have turned my thoughts to the better things of life. Harry— General Mendell, would you know what gives me the greatest satisfaction at this hour?"

"Yes, General Morgan."

"It is that I have always been true to others."

He cast his eye over the glittering assembly again.

"Harry—General Mendell, what gives *you* the most satisfaction to-night?"

"General Morgan, it is that I have always been true to *myself*."

As the assembly was about to dissolve, a lady in black approached General Harry Mendell, who was standing on the platform under the American flag, and said: "My father knew you, and he wished me some time to do you this honor. Will you allow me?"

She took from a faded piece of black velvet a small golden horseshoe and fastened it to his coat on the breast.

"My name is Fairfax, of the family of William Fairfax. This horseshoe, as I have been told its legend, was to be given to 'the most honorable rider.' I have heard your story and I think that it has found its true place—'To the most honorable rider.' "

A shout rose, filling the hall.

General Mendell was called upon to speak. He thought of the past and struggled against his emotions.

"My friends, I can only say that I have been true to the best that is in me, and it is because you have trusted me that my lady has put on my breast this." He touched the golden horseshoe and thought of his dead mother and wept.

The assembly stood silent before him.

CHAPTER XXV.

RECENTLY visited Greenway Court, the scene of this story, taking with me a photographer from Winchester, Va. I rode some ten miles over the hills of the Shenandoah to the White Post. Thence a mile or more to the old estate, a little off of the public way. The ride out of Winchester was most beautiful. Afar rose the verdant walls of the Blue Ridge, and among the valleys wound the clear Shenandoah. The farm-houses and barns were thrifty structures, and the orchards and wheat-fields indicated the salubrity of the climate and richness of the soil.

Arriving at the estate and seeing no long, rambling building, with great veranda and bell-towers, such as one might expect from the pictures in histories and cyclopædias, we asked a colored boy, lying in a woodpile:

"Where is Greenway Court?"

"Dun-no, sar: never heard of it befo', sar."

"But what place is this?"

"The Kennerly place, sar."

"Then it must be here."

"I live here, sar. Never heard of it befo'."

The estate was noble and worthy of the residence of a baron. It was circled by mountain walls, seen from the hills. A few miles away rolled the Indian Shenandoah. A long row of majestic locust trees led up to a new house that was made picturesque by airy porticoes. We saw a white man approaching and awaited his coming.

"Will you kindly tell us where Greenway Court was?"

"Right where you are, sir. The row of trees stood before the door."

"But where is the house now?"

"It has been taken down. I took it down myself, sir."

"Then, my good friend, you did a thing that the whole nation ought to regret."

"But the house was beyond repair, sir."

"Does nothing of it remain?"

"The little stone office yonder."

Near the house stood the white office that the old lord was accustomed to use in transacting legal business. Here Washington and young George Fairfax must have spent much time, and here Braddock may have studied the plans of his campaign with his officers, among them Washington and William Shirley, the son of the ex-Governor of Massachusetts who was known always in his last years as *Governor* Shirley.

We went to the white stone office. The door was closed. We knocked. The door was hurriedly opened, and in the sacred place we found three little negro boys shelling corn by the fire and keeping the fire alive by the cobs!

In front of the long row of grand decaying trees had stood the Court where the benevolent old Baron of Cameron used to entertain travellers like ourselves and fill the pockets of beggars with golden coins. Here the dream of Thackeray had seen the vision of the fiction of " The Virginians." Here, too, the fancies of John Esten Cooke had created a like fiction out of the old traditions. It was a place for fancy, legend, poetry, historic tales, and the painter's art.

We entered the new house. We were hospitably received and entertained, and were shown the calumet that old Lord Fairfax used to smoke in treaty-makings with the Indians. This we secured for the World's Columbian Exposition.

The old bells that had hung from the roof of the Court, to be rung in case of the approach of hostile Indians, had been disposed of; one of them had been given to a parish church. A few relics of the old lord's household effects remained, and we reported these to Mr. Curtis, of the Bureau of American Republics, Washington, in the interest of the World's Columbian Exposition.

As we stood under the great trees in the yard, a long vision of English history rose before us. The first, second, third, fourth, and fifth Lord Fairfax! We saw in fancy Nun-Appleton, the seat of the third Lord Fairfax, with its quaint peaked roofs and open court! Leeds Castle, Kent, the residence of the fifth Lord Fairfax, with stately towers reflected in the placid water. We heard resolute Lady Fairfax exclaim, when Charles I. was called upon to answer the charge of treason "in the name of all the good people of England": "It is a lie: not a hundredth part of them! *Oliver Cromwell is a traitor!*" We heard the marriage chimes of the fifth Lord Fairfax as he led to the altar Catharine, daughter of Lord Culpepper, or Colpepper, who inherited, besides Leeds Castle in Kent, the proprietary rights to some six million acres of land in Virginia.

It was Thomas, the son of this marriage, the sixth Lord Fairfax, who chose the Virginia estates for his disappointed life, and whose story we have in part told.

Out of his forest inheritance rose the multitudinous heroes of the glorious Shenandoah. The people of the valley ought never to have allowed the old Court to have gone out of repair or been taken down, for if the sixth Lord Fairfax was a Tory, his patriotism in the French and Indian war inspired and developed these young republican leaders whose immortal words and swords made America free.

We returned from Greenway Court to Winchester, to visit the tomb of the old lord, in the Winchester Episcopal church. He lies buried under the church, and his memorial tablets are seen in the church on the walls. Alone in his last sleep, even as he had lived much alone from the gay world, his name will ever re-call a generous and majestic memory, and he will be loved as one who exerted a noble influence on the character of young Washington, and through that influence helped to form for the American nation a hero for an eternal model who should receive the reverence of the ages.

This book is a fiction, yet founded largely on old traditions. It seeks to interpret through the creative fancy worthy men and deeds. If it have the influence that I desire, I shall be glad, my reader, that we have gone back to the past together and have visited in company old Lord Fairfax and the heroic Boys of Greenway Court.

APPENDICES.

APPENDIX A.

THE JOURNAL

OF

MAJOR GEORGE WASHINGTON,

SENT BY THE

Hon. ROBERT DINWIDDIE, Esqr.,

His Majesty's Lieutenant-Governor and
Commander-in-Chief of Virginia,

TO THE

COMMANDANT OF THE FRENCH FORCES

ON THE OHIO.

Wednesday, October 31st, 1753.

I WAS commissioned and appointed by the Honorable Robert Dinwiddie, Esq., Governor, &c., of Virginia, to visit and deliver a Letter to the Commandant of the French Forces on the Ohio, and set out on the intended journey the same Day: The next, I arrived at Fredericksburg, and engaged Mr. Jacob Vanbraam, to be my French Interpreter, and proceeded with him to Alexandria, where we provided Necessaries. From thence we went to Winchester, and got Baggage, Horses, &c., and from thence we pursued the new Road to Wills Creek, where we arrived the 14th of November.

Here I engaged Mr. Gist to pilot us out, and also hired

four others as Servitors, Barnaby Currin, and John Mac-
Guire, Indian Traders, Henry Steward, and William
Jenkins; and in Company with those Persons, left the In-
habitants the Day following.

The excessive Rains and vast Quantity of Snow which
had fallen, prevented our reaching Mr. Frazier's, an Indian Trader, at the Mouth of Turtle-Creek, on Monongahela (River) till Thursday the 22d. We were informed
here, that Expresses had been sent a few Days before to
the Traders down the River, to acquaint them with the
French General's Death, and the Return of the major
Part of the French Army into Winter Quarters.

The Waters were quite impassable without swimming
our Horses; which obliged us to get the Loan of a Canoe
from Frazier, and to send Barnaby Currin, and Henry
Steward, down the Monongahela, with our Baggage, to
meet us at the Forks of Ohio, about 10 Miles, there to
cross the Aligany. (The Ohio and Aligany are the same
River.)

As I got down before the Canoe, I spent some Time in
viewing the Rivers, and the Land in the Forks, which I
think extremely well situated for a Fort, as it has the ab-
solute Command of both Rivers. The Land at the Point
is 20 or 25 Feet above the common Surface of the Water;
and a considerable Bottom of flat, well-timbered Land all
around it, very convenient for Building: The Rivers are
each a Quarter of a Mile, or more, across, and run here
very near at right Angles: Aligany bearing N. E. and
Monongahela S. E. The former of these two is a very
rapid and swift running Water; the other deep and still,
without any perceptible Fall.

Adventures with the Chiefs Shingiss, of the Dela-
    wares, and Half-King, of the Six Nations—
    The "Speech-Belt."

About two Miles from this, on the South East Side of
the River, at the Place where the Ohio Company intended
to erect a Fort, lives Shingiss, King of the Delawares.
We called upon him, to invite him to Council at the
Loggs-Town.

As I had taken a good deal of Notice Yesterday of the
Situation at the Forks, my Curiosity led me to examine
this more particularly, and I think it greatly inferior,
either for Defence or Advantages; especially the latter:
For a Fort at the Forks would be equally well situated on
the Ohio, and have the entire Command of the Monongahela; which runs up to our Settlements and is extremely
well designed for Water Carriage, as it is of a deep still
Nature. Besides a Fort at the Fork might be built at a
much less Expence, than at the other place.

Nature has well contrived this lower Place for Water
Defence; but the Hill whereon it must stand, being about
a *quarter* of a Mile in Length, and then descending gradu-
ally on the *land* Side, will render it difficult and very ex-
pensive to make a sufficient Fortification there. The
whole Flat upon the Hill must be taken in, the Side next
the descent made extremely high, or else the Hill itself
cut away; *otherwise* the Enemy may raise Batteries within
that Distance without being exposed to a single *shot* from
the Fort.

Shingiss attended us to the Loggs-Town, where we arrived between Sun-setting and Dark, the 25th Day after I
left Williamsburg. We travell'd over some extreme good
and bad Land to get to this Place.

As soon as I came into Town, I went to Monakatoocha

19

(as the Half-King was out at his hunting Cabbin on Little Beaver Creek, about 15 Miles off), and informed him by John Davison, my Indian Interpreter, that I was sent a Messenger to the French General, and was ordered to call upon the Sachems of the Six Nations to acquaint them with it. I gave him a String of Wampum and a Twist of Tobacco, and desired him to send for the Half-King, which he promised to do by a Runner in the Morning, and for other Sachems. I invited him and the other great Men present to my Tent, where they stayed about an *hour*, and returned.

According to the best observations I could make, Mr. Gist's new settlement (which we passed by) bears about west northwest 70 miles from Will's Creek; Shannapins, or the Fork, N. by W. or North Northwest, about 50 Miles from that; and from thence to the Loggs-Town the course is nearly West about 18 or 20 Miles; So that the whole distance, as we went and computed it, is at least 135, or 140 miles from our back inhabitants.

25th. Came to town, four of ten Frenchmen, who had deserted from a company at the Kuskuskas, which lies at the mouth of this river. I got the following account from them. They were sent from New Orleans with 100 men, and 8 Canoe-loads of provisions to this place, where they expected to have met the same number of men, from the Forts on this side of Lake Erie, to convoy them and the stores up, who were not arrived when they ran off.

I inquired into the situation of the French on the Mississippi; their numbers, and what forts they had built. They informed me that there were four small forts between New Orleans and the Black Islands, garrisoned with about 30 or 40 men and a few small pieces in each. That at New Orleans, which is near the mouth of the Mississippi, there are 35 companies of 40 men each, with a pretty strong fort mounting 8 carriage guns; and at the Black Islands there are several companies, and a fort with six guns.   The Black Islands are about 130 leagues above the mouth of the Ohio, which is about three hundred and fifty above New Orleans.   They also acquainted me that there was a small palisaded fort on the Ohio, at the mouth of the Obaish, about 60 leagues from the Mississippi.   The Obaish heads near the West end of Lake Erie, and affords the communication between the French on the Mississippi and those on the lakes.   These deserters came up from the lower Shanoah town with one Brown, an Indian trader, and were going to Philadelphia.

About three o'clock this evening, the Half-King came to town.   I went up and invited him, with Davison, privately to my tent, and desired him to relate some of the particulars of his journey to the French commandant, and of his reception there.   Also, to give me an Account of the ways and distance.   He told me that the nearest and levelest way was now impassable, by reason of many large, miry savannas; that we must be obliged to go by Venango, and should not get to the near fort under 5 or 6 nights' sleep, good travelling.   When he went to the fort, he said he was received in a very stern manner by the late commander, who asked him very abruptly what he had come about, and to declare his business, which he said he did in the following speech:

"Fathers, I am come to tell you your own speeches, what your own mouths have declared.

"Fathers, you, in former days, set a silver basin before us, whereon there was a leg of beaver, and desired all the nations to come and eat of it, to eat in peace and plenty, and not to be churlish to one another; and that if any such person should be found to be a disturber, I here lay down by the edge of the dish a rod, which you must scourge them with; and if your father should get foolish, in my old days, I desire you may use it upon me as well as others.

"Now, fathers, it is you who are the disturbers in this land, by coming and building your towns, and taking it away unknown to us, and by force.

"Fathers, we kindled a fire a long time ago at a place called Montreal, where we desired you to stay, and not to come and intrude upon our land. I now desire you may dispatch to that place; for be it known to you, fathers, that this is our land, and not yours.

"Fathers, I desire you may hear me in civilness; if not, we must handle that rod which was laid down for the use of the obstreperous. If you had come in a peaceable manner, like our brothers the English, we would not have been against your trading with us; as they do but to come, fathers, and build houses upon our land, and to take it by force, is what we cannot submit to.

"Fathers, both you and the English are white, we live in a country between; therefore, the land belongs to neither one nor the other. But the Great Being above allowed it to be a place of residence for us; so, fathers, I desire you to withdraw, as I have done our brothers the English, for I will keep you at arm's length. I lay this down as a trial for both, to see which will have the greatest regard to it, and that side we will stand by, and make equal sharers with us. Our brothers the English, have heard this, and I come now to tell it to you, for I am not afraid to discharge you off this land."

This, he said, was the substance of what he spoke to the general, who made this reply:

"Now, my child, I have heard your speech. You spoke first, but it is my time to speak now. Were is my wampum that you took away with the marks of towns on it? This wampum I do not know, which you have discharged me off the land with; but you need not put yourself to the trouble of speaking, for I will not hear you. I am not afraid of flies or mosquitoes, for Indians are such as those. I tell you down that river I will go, and will build upon it, according to my command. If the river was blocked up, I have forces sufficient to burst it open, and tread under my feet all that stand in opposition, together with their alliances; for my force is as the sand upon the sea-shore; therefore, here is your wampum. I sling it at you. Child, you talk foolish; you say this land belongs to you, but there is not the black of my nail yours. I saw that land sooner than you did; before the Shannoahs and you were at war. Lead was the man who went down and took possession of that river. It is my land, and I will have it, let who will stand up for, or say against it. I will buy and sell with the English (mockingly). If people will be ruled by me, they may expect kindness, but not else."

The Half-King told me he had inquired of the general after two Englishmen who were made prisoners, and received this answer:

"Child, you think it a very great hardship that I made prisoners of those two people at Venango. Don't you concern yourselves with it, we took and carried them to Canada, to get intelligence of what the English were doing in Virginia."

He informed me that they had built two forts, one on Lake Erie, and another on French Creek, near a small lake, about fifteen miles asunder, and a large wagon-road between. They are both built after the same model, but different in size; that on the lake the largest. He gave me a plan of them of his own drawing.

The Indians inquired very particularly after their brothers in Carolina gaol.

They also asked what sort of a boy it was who was taken from the South Branch; for they were told by some Indians that a party of French Indians had carried a white boy by Kuskuska Town, toward the lakes.

November 26th. We met in council at the long-house about nine o'clock, when I spoke to them as follows:

"Brothers, I have called you together in council, by order of your brother, the Governor of Virginia, to acquaint you that I am sent with all possible dispatch to visit and deliver a letter to the French commandant, of very great importance to your brothers the English; and I dare say to you, their friends and allies.

"I was desired, brothers, by your brother, the Governor, to call upon you, the sachems of the nations, to inform you of it, and to ask your advice and assistance to proceed the nearest and best road to the French. You see, brothers, I have gotten thus far on my journey.

"His Honour likewise desired me to apply to you for some of your young men to conduct and provide provisions for us on our way, and be a safeguard against those French Indians who have taken up the hatchet against us. I have spoken thus particularly to you, brothers, because his Honour, our Governor, treats you as good friends and allies, and holds you in great esteem. To confirm what I have said, I give you this string of wampum."

After they had considered for some time on the above discourse, the Half-King got up and spoke:

"Now, my brothers, in regard to what my brother the Governor has desired of me, I return this answer:

"I rely upon you as a brother ought to do, as you say we are brothers, and one people. We shall put heart in hand and speak our fathers, the French, concerning the speech they made to me; and you may depend that we will endeavor to be your friend.

"Brothers, as you have asked my advice, I hope you will be ruled by it, and stay until I can provide a company to go with you. The French Speech-Belt is not here; I have to go for it to my hunting-cabbin. Likewise, the people whom I have ordered in are not yet come, and cannot until the third night from this; until which time, brother, I must beg you to stay.

"I intend to send the guard of Mingoes, Shannoahs, and Delawares, that our brothers may see the love and loyalty we bear them."

As I had orders to make all possible dispatch, and waiting here was very contrary to my inclination, I thanked him in the most suitable manner I could, and told him that my business required the greatest expedition, and would not admit of that delay. He was not well pleased that I should offer to go before the time he had appointed, and told me that he could not consent to our going without a guard, for fear some accident should befall us and draw reflection upon him. "Besides," said he, "this is a matter of no small moment, and must not be entered into without due consideration: for I intend to deliver up the French Speech-Belt, and make the Shannoahs and Delawares do the same." And accordingly he gave orders to King Shingiss, who was present, to attend on Wednesday night with the wampum; and two men of their nation to be in readiness to set out with us the next morning. As I found it was impossible to get off without affronting them in the most egregious manner, I consented to stay.

I gave them back a string of wampum which I met with at Mr. Frazier's, and which they sent with a speech to his Honour the Governor, to inform him that three nations of French-Indians,—namely, Chippoways, Ottaways, and Orundaks—had taken up the hatchet against the English; and desired them to repeat it over again. But this they postponed doing until they met in full council with the Shannoah and Delaware chiefs.

Nov. 27th. Runners were dispatched very early for the Shannoah chiefs. The Half-King set out himself to fetch the French Speech-Belt from his hunting-cabbin.

Nov. 28th. He returned this evening, and came with Monakatovcha and two other sachems to my tent and begged (as they had complied with his Honour the Governor's request, in providing men, etc.) to know on what business we were going to the French. This was a question I had all along expected, and had provided as satisfactory answers as I could; which allayed their curiosity a little.

Monakatovcha informed me that an Indian from Venango brought news a few days ago that the French had called all the Mingoes, Delawares, etc., together at that place, and told them that they intended to have been down the river this fall, but the waters were growing cold and the winter advancing, which obliged them to go into quarters; but that they might assuredly expect them in the spring with a far greater number; and desired that they might be quite passive and not intermeddle unless they had a mind to draw all their force upon them; for that they expected to fight the English three years (as they supposed there would be some attempts made to stop them), in which time they should conquer. But that if they should prove equally strong, they and the English would join to cut them all off, and divide the land between them; that though they had lost their general and some few of their soldiers, yet there were men enough to reinforce them, and make them masters of the Ohio.

This speech, he said, was delivered to them by one Captain Joncaire, their interpreter-in-chief, living at Venango and a man of note in the army.

Nov. 29th. The Half-King and Monakatovcha came

very early, and begged me to stay one day more; for not-withstanding they had used all the diligence in their power, the Shannoah chiefs had not brought the wampum they ordered, but would certainly be in to-night; if not, they would delay me no longer, but would send it after us as soon as they arrived. When I found them so pressing in their request, and knew that the returning of wampum was the abolishing of agreements, and giving this up was shaking off all dependence upon the French, I consented to stay, as I believed that an offence offered at this crisis might be attended with greater ill-consequence than an-other day's delay. They also informed me that Shingiss could not get in his men, and was prevented from coming himself by his wife's sickness (I believe by fear of the French), but that the wampum of that nation was lodged with Kustalogo, one of their chiefs, at Venango.

In the evening late, they came again, and acquainted me that the Shannoahs were not yet arrived, but that it should not retard the prosecution of our journey. He de-livered in my hearing the speech that was to be made to the French by Jeskakake, one of their old chiefs, which was giving up the belt the late commandant had asked for, and repeating nearly the same speech he himself had done before.

He also delivered a string of wampum to this chief, which was sent by King Shingiss, to be given to Kustalogo, with orders to repair to the French and deliver up the wampum.

He likewise gave a very large string of black and white wampum, which was to be sent up immediately to the Six Nations, if the French refused to quit the land at this warning, which was the third and last time, and was the night of this Jeskakake to deliver.

Nov. 30th. Last night, the great men assembled at

their council-house, to consult further about this journey, and who were to go; the result of which was, that only three of their chiefs, with one of their best hunters, should be our convoy. The reason they gave for not sending more, after what had been proposed at council the 26th, was, that a greater number might give the French suspicions of some bad design, and cause them to be treated rudely; but I rather think they could not get their hunters in.

We set out about nine o'clock with the Half-King, Jeskakake, White Thunder, and the Hunter; and travelled on the road to Venango, where we arrived the 4th of December, without anything remarkable happening but a continued series of bad weather.

Dec. 6th the Half-King came to my tent quite sober, and insisted very much that I should stay & hear what he had to say to the French. I fain would have prevented him from speaking anything until he came to the commandant, but could not prevail. He told me that at this place a council fire was kindled, where all their business with these people was to be transacted, & that the management of the Indian affairs was left solely to Monsieur Joncaire. As I was desirous of knowing the issue of this, I agreed to stay; but sent our horses a little way up French Creek to raft over and encamp, which I knew would make it near night. About ten o'clock they met in council. The king spoke much the same as he had before done to the general; and offered the French speech-belt which had before been demanded, with the marks of four towns on it, which Monsieur Joncaire refused to receive, but desired him to carry it to the fort to the commander.

Dec. 7th. Monsieur La Force, commissary of the French stores, and three other soldiers, came over to accompany us up. We found it extremely difficult to get the Indians off today, as every stratagem had been used to prevent their going up with me. I had last night left John Davi(d)-son (the Indian interpreter) whom I had brought with me from town, and strictly charged him not to be out of their company, as I could not get them over to my tent; for they had some business with Kustalogo, chiefly to know why he did not deliver up the French speech-belt which he had in keeping; but I was obliged to send Mr. Gist over today to fetch them, which he did with great persuasion.

At twelve o'clock, we set out for the fort, and were prevented arriving there until the 11th by excessive rains, snows, and bad travelling through many mires and swamps; these we were obliged to pass to avoid crossing the creek, which was impassable, either by fording or rafting, the water was so high and rapid.

We passed over much good land since we left Venango, and through several extensive and very rich meadows, one of which, I believe, was nearly 4 miles in length, and considerably wide in some places.

Dec. 12th. I prepared early to wait upon the commander, and was received and conducted to him by the second officer in command. I acquainted him with my business, and offered him my commission and letter; both of which he desired me to keep until the arrival of Monsieur Reparti, captain at the next fort, who was sent for and expected every hour.

This commander is a knight of the military order of St. Louis, and named Legardeur de St. Pierre. He is an elderly gentleman, and has much the air of a soldier. He was sent over to take the command immediately upon the death of the late general, and arrived about 7 days before me.

At 2 o'clock the gentleman who was sent for arrived,

when I offered the letter, &c., again, which they received, and adjourned into a private apartment for the captain to translate, who understood a little English. After he had done it, the commander desired I would walk in and bring my interpreter to peruse and correct it; which I did.

Dec. 13th. The chief officers retired to hold a council of war, which gave me an opportunity of taking the dimensions of the fort, and making what observations I could.

It is situated on the south or west forks of French Creek, near the water; and is almost surrounded by the creek, and a small branch of it, which form a kind of island. Four houses compose the sides. The bastions are made of piles driven into the ground, standing more than 12 ft. above it, and sharp at top, with port-holes cut for cannon, and loop-holes for the small arms to fire through. There are 8 six-pound pieces mounted in each bastion, and one piece of four-pounds before the gate. In the bastions are a guard-house, chapel, doctor's lodging, and the commander's private store; round which are laid platforms for the cannon and men to stand on. There are several barracks without the fort, for the soldiers' dwellings, covered, some with bark and some with boards made chiefly of logs. There are also several other houses, such as stables, smith's shop, &c.

I could get no certain account of the number of men here; but, according to the best judgment I could form, there are a 100, exclusive of officers, of whom there are many. I also gave orders to the people who were with me to take an exact account of the canoes, which were hauled up to convey their forces down in the spring. This they did, and told 50 of birch bark, and 170 of pine, besides many others, which were blocked out, in readiness for being made.

Dec. 14th. As the snow increased very fast, and our

horses daily became weaker, I sent them off unloaded, under the care of Barnaby Currin and two others, to make all convenient dispatch to Venango, & there to wait our arrival if there was a prospect of the river's freezing; if not, then to continue down to Shannopin's Town, at the fork of the Ohio, & there to wait until we came to cross the Allegany, intending myself to go down by water, as I had the offer of a canoe or two.

As I found many plots concerted to retard the Indians' business, and prevent their returning with me, I endeavoured all that lay in my power to frustrate their schemes, and hurried them on to execute their intended design. They accordingly pressed for admittance this evening, which at length was granted them, privately, to the commander and one or two other officers. The Half-King told me that he offered the wampum to the commander, who evaded taking it, and made many fair promises of love and friendship; said he wanted to live in peace, & trade amicably with them as a proof of which, he would send some goods immediately down to the Loggs-Town for them. But I rather think the design of that is to bring away all our straggling traders they meet with, as I privately understood they intended to carry an officer with them. And what rather confirms this opinion, I was inquiring of the commander by what authority he had made prisoners of several of our English subjects. He told me that the country belonged to them; that no Englishman had a right to trade upon those waters; and that he had orders to make every person prisoner who attempted it on the Ohio, or the waters of it.

I inquired of Captain Reparti about the boy that was carried by this place, as it was done while the command devolved on him, between the death of the late general, and the arrival of the present. He acknowledged that a boy had been carried past; and that the Indians had two or three white men's scalps, (I was told by some of the Indians at Venango, eight) but pretended to have forgotten the name of the place where the boy came from, & all the particular facts, though he had questioned him for some hours as they were carrying him past. I likewise inquired what they had done with John Trotter and James M'Clocklan two Pennsylvania traders, whom they had taken with all their goods. They told me that they had been sent to Canada, but were now returned home.

This evening I received answer to his Honour the Governor's letter from the commandant.

Dec. 15th. The commandant ordered a plentiful store of liquor and provision to be put on board our canoes, and appeared to be extremely complaisant, though he was exerting every artifice which he could invent to set our Indians at variance with us, to prevent their going until after our departure; presents, rewards, & everything which could be suggested by him or his officers. I cannot say that ever in my life I suffered so much anxiety as I did in this affair. I saw that every stratagem which the most fruitful brain could invent was practised to win the Half-King to their interest, and that leaving him there was giving them the opportunity they aimed at. I went to the Half-King and pressed him in the strongest terms to go; he told me that the commandant would not discharge him until the morning. I then went to the commandant, and desired him to do their business, and complained of ill treatment; for keeping them, as they were part of my company, was detaining me. This he promised not to do, but to forward my journey as much as he could. He protested he did not keep them, but was ignorant of the cause of their stay, though I soon found it out. He had promised them a present of guns, if they would wait until the morning. As I was very much pressed by the Indians to wait this day for them, I consented, on a promise that nothing should hinder them in the morning.

Dec. 16th. The French were not slack in their inventions to keep the Indians this day also. But as they were obliged, according to promise, to give the present, they then endeavoured to try the power of liquor, which I doubt not would have prevailed at any other time than this; but I urged and insisted with the King so closely upon his word that he refrained, and set off with us as he had engaged.

A Terrible Journey in Christmas Weather.

We had a tedious and very fatiguing passage down the creek. Several times we had liked to have been stayed against rocks; and many times were obliged all hands to get out and remain in the water half an hour or more, getting over the shoals. At one place, the ice had lodged and made it impassable by water; we were therefore obliged to carry our canoe across the neck of land, a quarter of a mile over. We did not reach Venango until the 22nd, where we met with our horses.

This creek is extremely crooked. I dare say the distance between the fort and Venango cannot be less than 130, to follow the meanders.

Dec. 23rd. When I got things ready to set off, I sent for the Half-King to know whether he intended to go with us or by water. He told me that White Thunder had hurt himself much, and was sick and unable to walk; therefore he was obliged to carry him down in a canoe. As I found he intended to stay here a day or two, and knew that Monsieur Joncaire would employ every scheme to set him against the English, as he had before done, I told him I hoped he would guard against his flattery, and let no fine

speeches influence him in their favour. He desired I
might not be concerned, for he knew the French too well
for anything to engage him in their favour; and that though
he could not go down with us, he yet would endeavour to
meet at the Forks with Joseph Campbell to deliver a speech
for me to carry to his Honour the Governor. He told me
he would order the young Hunter to attend us, and get
provisions, &c., if wanted.

Our horses were now so weak and feeble, and the baggage so heavy (as we were obliged to provide all the necessaries which the journey would require), that we doubted
much their performing it. Therefore, myself and others,
except the drivers, who were obliged to ride, gave up our
horses for packs, to assist along with the baggage. I put
myself in an Indian walking-dress, and continued with
them three days, until I found there was no probability of
the getting home in any reasonable time. The horses
became less able to travel every day; the cold increased
very fast; and the roads were becoming much worse by
a deep snow, continually freezing; therefore, as I was uneasy to get back, to make report of my proceedings to his
Honour the Governor, I determined to prosecute my journey the nearest way through the woods on.

Accordingly, I left Mr. Van Braam in charge of our
baggage, with money and directions to provide necessaries
from place to place for themselves and horses, and to make
the most convenient dispatch in travelling.

Dec. 26th. I took my necessary papers, pulled off my
clothes, and tied myself up in a watch-coat. Then, with
gun in hand and pack on my back, in which were my
papers and provisions, I set out with Mr. Gist, fitted in
the same manner, on Wednesday, the 26th. The day following, just after we had passed a place called Murdering
Town (where we intended to quit the path and steer

across the country for Shannopin's Town), we fell in with
a party of French Indians, who had lain in wait for us.
One of them fired at Mr. Gist or me, not 15 steps off,
but fortunately missed. We took this fellow into custody,
and kept him till about 9 o'clock at night, then let
him go, and walked all the remaining part of the night
without making any stop, that we might get the start so
far as to be out of the reach of their pursuit the next day,
since we were well assured they would follow our track as
soon as it was light. The next day we continued travelling
until quite dark, and got to the river about 2 miles above
Shannopin's. We expected to have found the river frozen,
but it was not, only about 50 yards from each shore.
The ice, I suppose, had broken up above, for it was drift-
ing in vast quantities.

There was no way of getting over but on a raft, which
we set about with but one poor hatchet, and finished just
after sun-setting. This was a whole day's work; we next
got it launched, then went on board of it and set off; but
before we were half way over, we were jammed in the
ice in such a manner that we expected every moment our
raft to sink, and ourselves to perish. I put out my setting-
pole to try to stop the raft that the ice might pass by,
when the rapidity of the stream threw it with so much
violence against the pole that it jerked me out into ten
feet of water; but I fortunately saved myself by catching
hold of one of the raft-logs. Notwithstanding all our efforts, we could not get to either shore, but were obliged,
as we were near an island, to quit our raft and make to it.

The cold was so extremely severe that Mr. Gist had all
his fingers, and some of his toes frozen; and the water was
shut up so hard that we found no difficulty in getting off
the island on the ice in the morning, and went to Mr.
Frazier's. We met here with 20 warriors, who were

20

going to the southward to war; but coming to a place on the head Great Kenhawa, where they found 7 people killed and scalped (all but one woman with very light hair), they turned about and ran back, for fear the inhabitants should rise and take them as the authors of the murder. They report that the bodies were lying about the house, and some of them much torn and eaten by the hogs. By the marks which were left, they say, they were French Indians of the Ottoway nation who did it.

As we intended to take horses here, and it required some time to find them, I went up about 3 miles to the mouth of Youghiogany, to visit Queen Aliquippa, who had expressed great concern that we passed her in going to the fort. I made her a present of a watch-coat and a bottle of rum, which latter was thought much the better present of the two.

Tuesday, the 1st of January. We left Mr. Frazier's house, and arrived at Mr. Gist's, at Monongahela, the 2nd, where I bought a horse and saddle. The 6th, we met 17 horses loaded with materials and stores for a fort at the Fork of the Ohio, and the day after some families going out to settle. This day we arrived at Will's Creek, after as fatiguing a journey as it is possible to conceive, rendered so by excessive bad weather. From the 1st day of December to the 15th, there was but one day on which it did not rain or snow incessantly; and throughout the whole journey we met with nothing but one continued series of cold, wet weather, which occasioned very uncomfortable lodgings, especially after we had quitted our tent, which was some screen from the inclemency of it.

On the 11th, I got to Belvoir, where I stopped one day to take necessary rest, and then set out and arrived in Williamsburg the 16th, when I waited upon his Honour the Governor, with the letter I had brought from the

French commandant, and to give an account of the success of my proceedings. This I beg leave to do by offering the foregoing narrative, as it contains the most remarkable occurrences which happened in my journey.

I hope what has been said will be sufficient to make your Honour satisfied with my conduct, for that was my aim in undertaking the journey, and chief study throughout the prosecution of it.

APPENDIX B.

THE character of Reuben Rouzé in this story is founded on the following true story of Reuben Rouzy:

"WASHINGTON'S DEBTOR.—One Reuben Rouzy, of Virginia, owed the general about one thousand pounds While President of the United States one of his agents brought an action for the money; judgment was obtained and execution issued against the body of the defendant, who was taken to jail. He had a considerable landed estate, but this kind of property cannot be sold in Virginia for debts unless at the discretion of the person. He had a large family, and for the sake of his children preferred lying in jail to selling his land A friend hinted to him that probably General Washington did not know anything of the proceeding, and that it might be well to send him a petition, with a statement of the circumstances. He did so, and the very next post from Philadelphia, after the arrival of his petition in that city, brought him an order for his immediate release, together with a full discharge and a severe reprimand to the agent for having acted in such a manner. Poor Rouzy was, in consequence, restored to his family, who never laid down their heads at night without presenting prayers to Heaven for their

'beloved Washington.' Providence smiled upon the
labors of the grateful family, and in a few years Rouzy
enjoyed the exquisite pleasure of being able to lay the
one thousand pounds, with the interest, at the feet of this
truly great man. Washington reminded him that the
debt was discharged. Rouzy replied the debt of his family
to the father of their country and preserver of their
parent could never be discharged; and the general, to
avoid the pressing importunity of the grateful Virginian,
who would not be denied, accepted the money, only, however, to divide it among Rouzy's children, which he immediately did."

APPENDIX C.

"Governor" Shirley.—His administration as Governor
of Massachusetts ended in 1745, but he still continued in
public life in the interest of the colony. He was ex-
governor at the time of this story.

APPENDIX D.

The story of the egg to be thrown at Warren was commonly known and believed in Boston, and has not been
disproved. It was a local story, but has been told in
history.

www.ingramcontent.com/pod-product-compliance
Lightning Source LLC
Chambersburg PA
CBHW060524030726
47498CB00004B/1070